THE MURIGRAM POST

THE MURIGRAM POST

A NOVEL

TAMAL MUKHERJEE

Highbrow Scribes Publications
New Delhi

Published by
HIGHBROW SCRIBES PUBLICATIONS
55-C, Jhang Appts., Sec.-13, Rohini, New Delhi
Mobile : +91-8826398333 +91-7982333488
E-mail : highbrowscribes@gmail.com

Website : www.highbrowscribes.com

First Published 2020

ISBN : 978-81-939504-7-0

Available Online
Amazon.in, Flipkart.com

Published in India by
Highbrow Scribes Publications

Typeset by Shagun Graphics, Delhi-110086
Cover Design by Disha Mukherjee & Anish Basu

Dedication

Mithu and Disha, for disagreeing with me

Mrini, for lighting up all my darkest hours

Author's Note

What began as a long novel ended up in a much shorter format. The reasons were many, partly arising out of my inability to deal with a blank, elastic canvas and partly due to the compulsions of keeping my job as a working journalist moving constantly from one emerging scenario to another. In a world caught in a perpetual motion of falling apart, I was trying to make a living pondering the banal, outlandish, nonsensical and the absurd. So, the days turned into weeks and months, and the half-finished chapters and sentences were left hanging.

Ultimately, someone close to me threatened, "Finish it in the next two months, or else..." The open-ended threat worked, and as a hardened hack, I kept to the deadline. That is, I overshot it by a mere two months and finally finished it in four. Someone, who I am very scared of, read the outcome and declared, "It has the right length, I went through it at one go." And so it went to the press.

To me, a novel is an intimate conversation with a close friend, perhaps on a rainy night, carried out over the dying flame of a candle where some strands are drowned out by the thunderstorm raging outside. But if she can catch a few words that transport her, even momentarily, to a world of heroic struggles and abysmal failures, I would consider myself lucky. As for the rest, it doesn't matter.

TAMAL MUKHERJEE

Chapter 1

Amal stubbed his twenty-first-and-a-half cigarette of the day in an earthen cup before deciding to make a move. It meant preparing himself mentally to get out of the raised wooden platform that served as a bed and face the wet dog whimpering in the corner.

This was a serious matter. First, as long as he was in the room, he would never willingly abandon his position. The bed was his sole property, his secure six by three feet that no one could lay claim to. Made from planks of soft, unseasoned *badam* wood nailed together, it was the most precious, coveted item in the room. The other three occupants of the walled space with a large rectangular gaping hole on one side that was meant to serve as a window eyed it jealously, with desire bordering on lust. It signified stature, position and power for whoever occupied it for whatever length of time. It commanded more respect than Amal's chair in the office.

The chair was usually taken by a person in charge of a shift. For most of the time, Amal would not sit on it, preferring to move around and, from time to time, capture any empty space that was available. This often meant perching himself on the table, on a pile of copy, covered with dust and ash spilt from overflowing burnt-clay teacups serving as ashtrays.

If Amal left the room even for a moment, to get a pack of cigarettes or tea from the roadside teashop, his place would surely be taken. A tussle ensued between Amal and the occupier of the wooden planks, which was finally settled through a compromise. Either Amal would agree to share his cup of tea or his cigarette that would be torn in half, or he would have to agree to wash blackish clothes hanging from a string tied to two nails on each side of the gaping hole in the wall.

The last option was the most fearsome. It was not the labour involved that worried Amal and two of the other inmates, but washing meant using the sole bar of all-purpose soap that had to be replaced by the person who used it up. The fourth inmate of the room, Pagla, was never a bathing and washing type, and no one could clearly remember when he had a bath last. Pagla survived on cigarettes, mostly borrowed from others, cups of tea bought on credit from Banshi's stall, and by simply gazing for hours at the ceiling and walls that had whitewash flaking off.

Pagla was an authority on the trajectory and final destination of whitewash flakes. He could predict accurately the time of day or night when a tiny scrap of hardened slaked lime would be dislodged from its distant moorings. He could chart its flight path and tell whether it would land in the newly bought cup of tea that was balanced delicately on top of a stack of books, dumped on a bundle of clothes that were meant to be worn to the office the next day. On such matters, Pagla's word was final. He could even decipher the progress of civilizations through the disintegration of spalling lime. The changing lines on the walls would refer to the decline of nations. The Soviet Union fell apart, and a new coalition of states emerged on the walls. Radcliff's Partition Line cut off one corner of the ceiling. The entire British Empire occupied the whole room.

ශ෴

One night, one tiny bit of cement and lime, spurred by a gust of wind, came to rest in Ranen's cup of tea.

'What the hell?' screamed Ranen, picking up the tea-soaked flake. 'Can't you see where the bastard is going?' He placed the cup under Pagla's nose.

This was a dangerous ploy at three thirty in the morning since tea was the elixir of life. But Ranen had perhaps taken the risk knowing it was Pagla whom he was challenging. Pagla would never really take anything by force or without asking someone for it. Not even a cigarette, which was the only thing he would ask for most of the time. He was the least violent, in fact, a pacifist among the four. He was secretly believed to be a saint by the other three.

'I had once secretly prayed to Pagla,' confessed Ranen. 'My rationale was if every man was divine, I might be able to touch Pagla's divinity since he is easily accessible.'

Amal lit a new cigarette, sending smoke rings of varying thickness and radii into the air.

'My prayer really worked since I had asked for the impossible,' Ranen continued. 'It was the day of the Tagore holiday. Only Pagla and I were left here manning the fort. Late that night, I decided to pray to Pagla when he was in a deep reverie. I prayed to him to ensure that Pradipta came back the next day for the night shift, which was asking for the moon.'

'I don't remember why I came back really,' Pradipta agreed, continuing his conversations with Baudelaire.

'The problem with Pagla's sainthood is he doesn't believe in anything, least of all God,' said Amal. 'He doesn't know if he could believe in anything at all.'

'It doesn't matter whether he believes or not. In fact, we all know that he is quite blank most of the times,' said Ranen. 'But I half-believed in him, and it worked. So, he must be close to being a saint.'

'Bastard!' shouted Pradipta, not explaining whether the comment was aimed at Pagla or Amal or Ranen or was simply meant as a compliment for one of his favourite poets. There were a few obscenities that Pradipta used both ways. 'Bastard' was the mildest among those that could mean that he held the recipient's illegitimacy in high esteem.

'If you think Pagla was behind granting your wish, you must give him a cigarette,' Amal pointed out.

'I gave him half a cigarette since it was kind of a half-wish,' argued Ranen, lighting a quarter of a cigarette that he had saved since morning.

Pagla wasn't around to contribute to his sainthood theory. Even if he were, he would most likely have kept silent, keeping his eyes focused on the transformations on the ceiling. In office, he hardly ever talked, except to ask the chief sub whether a story would go to page one or six. Apart from Ranen's secret admiration of Pagla, people knew that he was a solid sub. Both Amal and Pradipta respected him since he could work without uttering a word.

'You are the real bastards,' Ranen muttered, suddenly thinking of the work Pagla did. Ranen knew that apart from Amal and Pradipta, Pagla was considered a flawless editor. 'You exploit him knowing he is the weakest and won't protest.'

'Shut up, you are the weakest,' Pradipta said. 'How could you take the woman's picture on page one and shove the handshake to an inside page?'

Women were Ranen's weakest point. Amal had once found a picture hiding under Ranen's trousers. Though Ranen had protested that the picture was a laundry wrapper, he was stuck with the stigma for good. Even Pagla had made a rare comment that Ranen was 'soft at heart'.

'Don't talk about news,' Ranen thundered. 'You shoved the prime minister once to the sports page.'

'That was a matter of conviction, not lust, like in your case.'

'You don't have the capacity to lust and therefore you cling to a cigarette.'

Amal always enjoyed a fight between Pradipta and Ranen since victory inevitably depended on who was smoking a superior brand at that point in time.

Today Pradipta was the loser since Ranen still had one filter cigarette left in his pack and Pradipta was dragging on a hand-rolled local bidi.

'*Shaala*, give me a drag, at least,' Pradipta requested, throwing his Baudelaire down and throwing up his hands in a gesture of surrender.

Ranen gladly relented, handing over the freshly lit stick to Pradipta.

ఆ

These were the times Ranen relished the most. It was always difficult to win an argument with Pradipta, and when one did, the least one could do was to part with a cigarette. Pradipta's tenacity to hold on to a position, even a chair, was legendary. Once, Pradipta refused to get out of his chair in the office, and a couple of people got killed. Police did the killing, that is.

Amal never quite understood why Pradipta had made an issue of vacating his chair when his boss suddenly turned up at night. Pradipta was sacked, and the incident went a little too far, thought Amal. The boss walked out in a huff; the management issued a show-cause notice the next day, the employees mostly stood by the chief sub, who refused to budge from his ground of not budging from his chair. A face-saving apology was sought, and when it did not come, to save the boss's face, the chief sub was asked to go.

'It was the bastard's wife's face they were saving,' said Pradipta, not willing even after years to give up his right to the chair.

'Men have killed other men and done worse things over women's honour.'

'Never. They have fought over the perceived sense of their honour, which they never had. Honourable men don't fight. Putting up their mistresses to justify a weak case,' snapped Pradipta.

'Those who have honour never fight?' Amal egged on, not that he cared much about the line of argument, but he was always fascinated by the way Pradipta made his point.

He would stand up, pace up and down, and when one thought the debate had come to an end, he would sit down abruptly, saying, 'Shaala.'

The boss, he maintained, had felt a bit romantic on his day off and gone to see a film with his wife next door from the office. The film put him in a more romantic mood, and to get a bit of respect back from his wife, he wanted to show her how much respect he commanded in office. Hips swaying in unison like characters in the Hindi film they had just seen, the two, chewing paan after drinking lime juice, walked into a harassed newsroom already on nerve's edge trying to cope with a walkout in parliament.

Pradipta had not even looked up. That was his first offence. He also recognized, like everyone else, the boss's wife, but not the boss. That was the final straw. Seeing the matter getting out of his hands, the boss declared his prerogative and wanted to change the lead. Pradipta turned it down, arguing a Bihar lead on the day of a bloody battle in parliament would make the paper a laughing stock of the town.

Knowing he had already become a laughing stock of the newsroom, the boss tried to wrest control of the situation. He dived for the chair when the chief sub had half risen from it and, in the end, just managed to push the chief sub and the chair over. Pradipta had seen the boss coming, and being younger and fitter, he shoved his backside in to regain his position.

The truth was buried in the ensuing tussle. Journalists and employees said the boss had assaulted their boss. The boss and the management charged that it was a matter of the company's honour.

'It was a battle of bums, literally, though I didn't actually mind the bum shove,' Pradipta admitted. 'How can a paan-eating bastard grab an edition?'

Pradipta was always agitated about paan for some strange reason, Amal knew. He even pushed a pet theory that paan was one of the root causes of backwardness.

'It's the scarlet banner of feudalism. You eat paan and douse yourself in perfume when you go to a brothel.'

'What's a brothel got to do with paan?'

'Everything. The way it is made and served. Can you think of the nautch girls without paan and perfume? Even the girls had paan. The taste of *jarda* added to the allure of perfume acts as an aphrodisiac,' Pradipta continued, going into the intricacies of making different types of paan.

'It turns you on then.'

'It does. Have you had a paan with your girl? The juices, the chewed bits of the leaf, and the smells merge into one single whole. An aromatic coalescence of souls.'

'Don't have one yet,' Amal explained, meaning a girl.

'Ask her, "Would you like to have a paan?" Asking her for dinner is prehistoric. Sharing a paan is spiritual,' Pradipta carried on, assuming Amal was either lying about a girl or he would soon have one.

'These days you could try the chewing gum, I guess.'

'That's the problem with you,' Pradipta shot back, jumping up and starting to pace up and down again. 'You are too much of a postmodernist junkie to believe anything happened in the past.'

Amal loved Pradipta in this mood. He would run his fingers through his thick back-brushed hair, pick up another cigarette, and let it alternately dangle unlit from his lips and his clenched fist, and start reciting from Tagore.

Amal never failed to be amazed by what Pradipta believed in and how he acted. Despite being a rationalist like Amal himself, everything about Pradipta reminded one of the past. The way he combed his hair and especially the way he held his cigarette between the second and third finger and inhaled through a clenched fist. Amal once tried to do the same and ended up coughing, getting only a whiff of smoke since most of it escaped through the clenched fist.

'Despite your rabid anti-feudalism, you are an archetypal *babu*,' Amal pointed out. 'You smoke a fag as if you are drawing on a hookah!'

Nothing would unnerve Pradipta more than the babu bit. 'The hair and my smoking are my father's legacy. I am not a bastard like you are.'

Amal would leave it at that, enjoying the charged atmosphere and knowing that Pradipta's encounter with ancestral history was merely a long list of obscenities. But still, Pradipta had a point. Amal knew he was an extreme rationalist, perhaps to the point where rationalism was an end in itself. He would usually see Pradipta's point of view and also his and therefore never took a position on anything. His rationalism gave him a convenient excuse not to act. Pradipta plunged headlong into a crisis, even knowing that he would lose.

'How could you launch a strike because of a paan?'

'This modern obsession with cigarettes and liquor has killed sex,' Pradipta continued, ignoring Amal. 'It's been reduced to a drunken plunge, from what it was earlier, a magical game of enticement and submission.'

'Believe me, a bit of the chewed leaf was stuck on the bastard's lower lip and reeking of *attar* sold on the pavement, flashing crimson teeth and tongue, he said sorry. Show your red-hot lips to your wife, damn it.'

'You sure about the attar?' Amal, ever a non-paan-eating, non-attar-dousing journalist, tried to double-check.

'He's stingy as hell. Doesn't spend on anything else.'

ꕥ

Amal could never be sure about the perfume. It was not clear whether it was the boss's aftershave or his wife's perfume that had led to the ruckus. It could not be established whether anyone at all was smelling sweet or foul. Smell can be so much a state of the mind. In the heat and smoke generated by the paan and push, everyone smelt everything else. As a matter of fact, all the smells had sort of cancelled each other out in the end. The employees' lawyers argued in court that paan meant the boss was drunk and he was trying to hide the stink.

Experts were called in to testify as to the various kinds of smells and their effects on physiognomy. The management's lawyers showed the boss never used cheap perfume since his wife would never settle for it. Moreover, the smell of printer's ink was too strong at the time to have allowed any other stink to overwhelm it. Rickshaw pullers to bank officers to poets all vouched they had seen the boss, his wife, the chief sub, his colleagues, and everyone else drinking at a nearby country liquor store. The list of drunkards seen that night even included an employee who had died the previous year.

Whatever the smell was, the boss left the scene that night with his confused wife in tow. Two employees who were both off duty on the night of the disturbance were shot dead by police following a strike. The management sacked Pradipta and declared a lockout that lasted for 129 days.

'You won,' Amal agreed.

'Won the case but lost my chair.' Pradipta took a long drag on his Charminar and sat down again on the edge of the bed that Amal was occupying.

ꕥ

Chapter 2

The debate on the justification of a paan-driven strike took place long ago. Amal was stringing for a north-east newspaper, living in a room in a mess in Mandi bazaar, and Pradipta was unemployed and considered unemployable since he had won the case. He was simply smoking happily Amal's Charminars and reminding him that he must get some food from the canteen before it closed.

'If you don't get any grub now, both of us will starve.'

Amal was trying to calculate whether semi-starvation was better than being forced to cut down on cigarettes over the next few days. Though the month had ended, the cheque would not come in before the tenth—that too if he was lucky. Stringers were not considered top priority anywhere. And he knew Pradipta was totally broke.

'Goshtohhh?'

Goshto was a demigod to the mess inmates. He did everything from supplying hot water to polishing shoes to getting cigarettes. It was even possible, if one could keep Goshto happy, to make delayed payments at the mess. Everyone kept Goshto happy. They respected and, in some cases, revered him. He was their saviour. It didn't matter that Goshto couldn't read or write. What mattered was Goshto listened to all and tried to make everyone feel at home. And for most, the mess was better than home. The dark, damp, dingy smoke-filled environs of the Das Lodge rejuvenated them. There were no strangers there.

The rain continued like a nagging Manager-babu, slanting in through the worn-out bamboo blinds, knocking at each and every door down the veranda, and posting a wet note of ultimatum. As the puddles grew around the door frame in each room, the inmates knew it was Manager-babu's turn to play the boss. It was time to partly clear their monthly dues at the mess. During these days of the month, all would keep a low profile, smile graciously at Manager-babu, and some would even offer him a cigarette or two. Amal would inevitably ask Manager-babu about his wife's health.

'She has finally stopped taking the ruinous antibiotics and is feeling better. *Tulsi* leaves and honey, really. And she seems to be coping with the rains a lot better than last year.'

'But you must make sure she has a lot of vitamins,' said Amal, trying to be deeply concerned.

'The magic of tulsi, Amal-babu, the magic of tulsi. I know educated young people like you do not believe in ancient medicines anymore. But the first day she had the potion, she immediately got her voice back and was even humming a tune.'

Manager-babu began in earnest, recalling his first meeting with the girl he was about to marry. He had heard her sing but had not seen her face since it was impolite to look directly at a girl. And he loved her and married her. But the voice he loved was creating much of a problem these days because she had lost most of it for most of the year.

'But I can't make her stop eating sour chutney,' Manager-babu mumbled, losing his own voice at the end.

'You can't let her do that,' Amal agreed, slipping in a

fifty-rupee note under the red hard-bound register on the table. 'Haven't got my Jeep story cheque yet.'

Manager-babu merely nodded, by this time far withdrawn into his own ancient world of exotic leaves and bridal love songs.

◦◦◦

Health was a sure card one could play with Manager-babu. Those who entered the mess for the first time learnt its rules quickly enough. Their orientation started with Manager-babu's health, in fact. A new guest would sit quietly at Manager-babu's desk as he would explain how he won his battle for life. It had been a dark blustery night when he started oozing blood. He had been rushed to hospital in a three-wheeler where a young surgeon slit open his stomach and saved him. At this point, Manager-babu would stand up suddenly, unbutton his shirt and put his bisected stomach on display. If the new guest failed to show sufficient interest in the hairy, stitched-up belly, the chances were he would have only a slim chance of staying on at the mess. He would either be shunted to the room next to Goshto's where the ceiling leaked and the window frames were half-eaten by termites or he would be asked to pay his bills on time, which was even a more dreadful option than the first. In either case, he would be forced to leave. But those who came to the Das Lodge knew its rules by heart. And the expression of sympathy for a scarred stomach was absolutely no price at all. For the comforts that came with one's admission were countless.

Goshto was everyone's personal servant, mentor and friend. Just a shout was enough to get his attention, and most of the times it would be answered with a heavenly hot cup of tea. In times of illness, Manager-babu became one's father and friend. An ill man would get buttered toast for breakfast, fish at lunch and even chicken stew at dinner. Some days the fare would be topped with delicious rice pudding prepared by Manager-babu's wife. All inmates prayed to God that they would fall sick from time to time.

But those who lived at the Das Lodge were people far removed from sickness. Their bodies were tempered by roaming the dusty lanes of the town, breathing in unadulterated fumes from the snorting, puffing maze of trucks, cars, three-wheelers and scooters. Their minds were kept alert by the life-saving smoke of roasted and unroasted tobacco. Their spirit was sustained by a clash with a world that they did not belong to but fought every inch of the way. The tonnes of slag and ash from the plant beside the main road filled the air with a mist as if the whole town was going through an incessant eruption of joy, playing Holi with black powder. Hindi film songs gushed from shopfronts and speeding three-wheelers, pining for the return of the beloved.

Pradipta squeezed himself out of the three-wheeler, paying the driver with a new five-rupee note. He hated to part with it, knowing a crisp fiver could at least fetch one free Charminar from Banshi's shop. But he had no choice. This was the last piece of currency he had, and he needed to make the trip to Phulbazar to meet Majhi. He hated the meeting as well. It had nothing to do with Majhi, really. He, in fact, liked Majhi when he abused the plant and its bosses. Majhi had many stories, most of which could not be confirmed. Still Pradipta liked those, especially the one in which Majhi claimed to have put the MD Parekh in his place.

'I had a gulp of *chullu* before I stepped in that evening,' Majhi confessed. 'This guy had no business to be there. Parekh Sahab, why were you there, Parekh Sahab?'

Pradipta could not be sure how many times he had heard different versions of the incident. Each time it had a twist, but he could not care much since at the end of it, both of them would abuse Parekh together.

There was orgasmic pleasure in cursing Parekh. Pradipta would slip into Hindi as the tempo increased, while Majhi would switch to English even though he did not have a wide repertory of invectives in that language.

'The son of a bitch was caught in the park. My dad got him out because of the union boss,' said Majhi.

'Because of the flat,' corrected Pradipta.

Still, it didn't matter, really. It didn't matter that Pradipta would never meet Parekh face-to-face. Neither was it proven that Majhi had ever met the MD. What mattered was calling names to their hearts' content since everyone agreed Parekh was a rogue. He built the plant's golf course right through the slums.

The day the bulldozers came, Pradipta was part of the crowd, watching. A part of the crowd watched, too. The plant's PR man pushed through the crowd and reached for Pradipta.

'Sorry, boss, these guys were warned,' explained the PR man.

'Shaala,' said Pradipta.

Still, the shanties were razed. The little boy was crying all through the morning. Pradipta gave him fifty paise, and the crying stopped. The boy clutched his hands. 'Babu, give me two rupees. Haven't eaten for two days.'

ଔ

The watchful crowd merely displayed the tired interest of a resigned cognoscente. They looked like a newspaper drama critic watching a play put up by amateur actors from a neighbourhood club. They appeared like a panel of experts being shown a video presentation on the dangers of nuclear war. They all knew the script, every bit of it, even before the play had started.

'They had attained moksha in their past lives,' Pradipta later said one day. 'They had a renunciant's resignation even when their homes and lives were being systematically demolished by company thugs.'

'You believe in homes? A cluster of tarpaulin and tin shacks? These people have more sense than in our educated brains,' Amal countered.

'They could have at least shouted, screamed, done something,' Pradipta continued, knowing he had no argument at all.

'You mean you could have shouted, screamed, and done something, Pradipta, like the lone woman? You could have even written a fifty-buck piece for the regional pages in your paper—"Woman Killed at Shanty Dwellers' Peaceful Rally." Don't blame others for your inabilities.'

'I thought peace was your problem usually,' Pradipta hit back, 'not knowing when to support or oppose Gandhi. For you, peace is fine, so long as everyone gets quietly buried under the watchful eyes of the United Nations.'

'What could they have done? Submitted a memorandum

to the deputy commissioner? And you would have surely been roped in to draft that. That would have given you a good night's sleep.'

Amal was unusually harsh, even to the point of making a personal attack. This was indeed a rare Amal. Pradipta knew Amal never got angry while arguing. Rationality was Amal's cover, but even he couldn't hide the pain at times. It was as if the voicelessness and paralysis affected Amal more than Pradipta or even the slum dwellers. Amal fell silent.

Pradipta walked up to him, grasped his shoulder, and offered a cigarette. Both men turned their faces away from each other. The silence of the room was deepened by the intrusion of a faint song drifting in from a distant transistor.

Chapter 3

They all stood silently since there was nothing else to do. Three trucks were lined up. A couple of police jeeps blared crackling warnings that merged with film songs delivered from a microphone fixed to a car. Two pot-bellied plain-clothes cops in dhotis and half-sleeved shirts waved their revolvers, screaming abuses at whoever stepped close.

Only a woman whose sari had come off and whose blouse was ripped in half was rolling on the ground. She was oblivious to what was going on. One dhoti-clad cop got hold of both her hands and twisted them behind her back. He struggled to lift her from the ground. One pert, firm breast broke free, while a part of the torn blouse covered the other.

Pradipta couldn't help being stunned by her beauty. Wet strands of curly long hair plastered her deep-set black eyes. But she was in a trance, unable to see what was going on. Only her voice rose above all obstacles, heavenwards. Pradipta had never known such dignity. The other cop clutched the woman's leg and dragged her towards a jeep.

She had nothing to hide by now. The torn dark-green blouse was hanging from her shoulder. The dirt-covered grey petticoat was pulled back to her waist. The cop was using the petticoat as a kind of rope around her waist and was dragging her and her left leg by it. She managed to turn her head and sink her teeth into the arms of the cop who was twisting her arms behind her back.

'Whore. You deserve to die!' screamed the cop. The face turned upwards; the eyes opened for a moment before closing after the butt of the revolver hit the skull. As the dark red fluid covered the side of her face, she ceased to struggle any more.

This was one of the very few occasions when Pradipta gave anyone any money without him earning it. His point always was, 'the poor must protest.' And of course, fifty paise would have been well spent on tea or cigarettes. He gave the boy tugging at his shirt the coin and pushed him away.

They mostly stood watching silently, as if Parekh were delivering the efficiency pitch at the boardroom. A few would ask the known questions, to be followed by the known replies.

'Has anyone told Ismael?'

'Hari's gone to the hospital. But they haven't released her body yet.'

'Will Hari tell him?'

'About what?'

'About his house?'

'His shack?'

'That was at least better than Parekh's.'

'How do you know? No one saw the place.'

'The room was full of water, like the ones you see in films. I almost went down with the TV into the pond in the room. Luckily, it wasn't deep.'

'I think Hari will tell him. And also, it's better to lose all at one go—shack and wife.'

'I gave Parekh two bucks actually and asked him to fetch cigarettes,' claimed Majhi.

'You can check it out with Manoj and others, they were all there on the shop floor that evening.'

Pradipta never checked it out. He didn't care if it actually happened. There were some things that shouldn't be checked out, like love, Pradipta knew. You must believe in it and it would grow. As long as someone professed love and was willing to die for it, the truth would stay unsullied. Checking brings in that element of uncertainty, which changes the whole story. It's like Heisenberg's uncertainty principle. Love, like that elusive unseen particle, can never be quantified in any time and place.

'But the particle is true, even if you can't put your finger on it,' Amal said. 'You don't have to see something to know it exists.'

'It may exist in your mind. It perhaps has use for guys like you who stay enclosed in their minds forever.'

'You can't deny the existence of love, be it in the mind or heart or wherever. What's important is its efficacy,' Amal fought back. 'For you, you are doing something to show love. For me, I profess it.'

'I don't show love at all. I show work, I live and die in work. If someone believes I love her, that's her illusion.'

'You believed Shantheni was tending to believe she loved you.'

'Shut up!' Pradipta shouted, as if Amal was proving to be completely unscrupulous.

Amal was not quite sure if Pradipta didn't really believe in love or if he was somehow scared. Perhaps he could deal with friends or opponents, and he didn't know what to do with friends who frequently turned opponents. That's what happened in love. There are no friends or opponents; they both merge into one.

'Why is it two people who are in love are always hated by others?' Pradipta continued. 'Why is it they themselves hate others when they say love transforms people?'

'We aren't perfect. Love is such an attraction since it creates the aura of perfection.'

'This is no argument at all, this is primary school stuff. We live in a morass of imperfection, bouncing back and forth between different levels of imperfection. In fact, perfection is less imperfection anyway, unless you are talking of God.'

'Why can't we talk of God then?'

'Why should God be hated then and get crucified?'

'We are simply scared.'

'Or there is nothing called human love. All those guys who were driving the nails were professing love to their girlfriends and mistresses. *Love* by your definition has to be exclusive. It must preclude hatred, jealousy, and the rest. Or else, it is something else, like the lust I trust so much.' Pradipta took another cigarette from Amal's pack as if it was his right to do so.

'It is so easy to understand you from the point of view of an ascetic. You are the most wonderful atheist believer I have ever seen. You will end up joining an ashram,' said Amal, taking his pack back and putting it in his pocket.

'Why should I become a renunciant? I don't believe in God.' Pradipta was curious.

'You believe in absolutes. Perfection.'

☙

These were times Pradipta would find it hard to argue with Amal. The structure of Amal's logic fascinated him. The consistency, cohesion and beauty were enthralling. Amal could start arguing about a front-page headline and very soon conclude that the headline giver had egg curry for lunch at the dhaba. Pradipta knew he could only attack the hypothesis, the premises upon which Amal had built his thesis, but never its logical consistency.

But there was no need for logic with Majhi. All he needed was mollycoddling and the hurling of joint abuses at the plant. Today, Pradipta thought, he needed to raise the level of abuses since he needed the cheque. It was not Majhi's fault, though. His bosses in the capital didn't care about the desperation of a freelancer trying not to be thrown out by Manager-babu. For that matter, they didn't care about any freelancer at all. He hadn't come across a single freelancer who had been paid in full, let alone been paid on time. Majhi had sent three same telex messages: 'Pradipta's Chex Pending Pl Do Needful Rgds.'

There was only one reply that the needful was being done: 'Bijoy-babu Back Friday Rgds.'

There was so much regard for each other in telex, Pradipta wondered. And all these guys wouldn't even interrupt their midday meals if you died in the office drain.

It was once raining heavily. In fact, it had been raining

for the past three days. The city was flooded by the time Pradipta waded through knee-deep water to reach the head office. By late evening, the water had risen up to the first intersection of the main collapsible gate. The rain poured incessantly like slogan-shouting at a party rally, drenching and sickening even those who tried to stay away from its line of outburst. It slanted in through the broken glass patched up with a newspaper on a window near the ceiling. The crowd swelling at the gate did not care about the water from above. They were watching if the force was easing, if they could somehow step into the dark currents flowing through the lane.

Pradipta was debating whether to give it a shot as well. He wanted to go to the railway station and spend the night there. He had to catch the first morning train. He hated spending the night in the office with a crowd he despised from the bottom of his heart. This was a group of people who believed they were journalists, but they never ever cared about a story. They sat up there in the reporting room, calling up the police control room and party bosses, and banging their stories out on three sheets of paper, with two carbon papers slipped in.

'The girl's dead, Tarunda, the girl's dead,' pleaded Pradipta. 'She was returning from school with her mother when the firing began.'

'Can't help it,' explained Tarun. 'The rally speech must be on page one. And the police are claiming there were a few injuries and no deaths.'

'She was ten years old, and they tried to hide inside the tailor's shop. The tailor tried to put up the planks. But one bullet hit her. She died on her mother's lap.'

'Sorry,' Tarun said, unrelenting. 'If you are interested in it, give just three paras for page seven. But you have to state that unconfirmed reports say one girl died in the firing.'

'Unconfirmed?' Pradipta asked. 'I saw the body at her home. Her mother has gone berserk.'

'We can't ascribe the death to police firing unless they confirm that. And how do you know she died from police bullets?'

'How do you know you are not the chief minister?' Pradipta walked out.

Pradipta was thinking of walking out in the rain when a young typesetter took the first step into the unknown. All phones were dead in the office. He didn't know how his wife was coping since their tiny two rooms in the refugee colony were likely to be in the middle of an ocean. As he moved towards the other side of the lane which had become a deadly canal of fast-flowing water, a blinding flash lit up his face. The submerged electric box also became visible for a brief moment. He shrieked; his body convulsed before he went inside the water. The body kept floating in the lane for hours since no one else could risk bringing it back to the office.

ʚɞ

Chapter 4

'Shaala,' mumbled Pradipta, since it was Friday, and his life depended on Bijoy-babu's descent. Bijoy-babu lived in what was known as a posh company flat on the top floor of the office block. If he didn't come to work, it meant he hadn't taken the flight of stairs down to the floor below.

Bijoy-babu was extremely hard to get, even though nobody had ever seen him leave the office building. Security guard Moloy, who had been working in the office for thirty-three years, maintained the accounts manager hadn't left the building in the last three decades. Still, it was not easy to get Bijoy-babu to sign on anything. He had so many papers to sign. All vouchers had to be passed by him; all cheques had to bear his signature. Once, Rathindranath ran a signature campaign, protesting against the decision to build a road through his twenty-hectare estate in Parashitola. Close to fifty thousand signatures were collected, and the road was never built. It was widely believed most of the signatures were given by Bijoy-babu under different names. Moloy said he ran up and down the stairs to collect the sheaves of papers.

'Bijoy-babu was doing it all alone upstairs. Rathindranath was hovering over him. And they had run out of names a long time ago. I gave them the names of all my ancestors I could think of,' Moloy said.

'What about addresses?' asked Pradipta.

'It didn't matter. They kept putting hundreds in one locality.'

'I simply hope Bijoy signs my cheque today,' Pradipta told Amal before he left the mess. 'And the courier has to pick it up before four.'

'Even then you wouldn't be sure that the piece of paper would reach you tonight.' Amal was simply being his usual sceptical self.

'I will break the boy's legs if he smokes ganja again and doesn't turn up.' Pradipta appeared determined since he knew that even though Amal's generosity was infinite, he couldn't depend on it infinitely long. 'I will take the next train to head office and take Bijoy's dhoti off if he doesn't sign it today.'

Amal knew Pradipta was quite capable of that, and he knew that Bijoy-babu knew that as well. That was why Bijoy-babu never kept Pradipta waiting too long. A third reminder was perhaps the maximum leeway Bijoy-babu had. Pradipta had once gone in search of Bijoy-babu. Majhi promptly sent a telex that Pradipta was on his way.

Bijoy-babu was laid up upstairs with a particularly serious attack of piles. He had, in fact, cancelled two meetings with the union even though the bonus had to be declared in another seven days. Bijoy-babu came down that day. He signed the cheque for Pradipta and held a long meeting with the union.

'Pradipta-babu, you must come down here before the bonus negotiations. Bijoy really doesn't want his dhoti taken off,' union president Sadhan Pakrashi said.

'Why can't you guys take his dhoti off if you think the

threat to his attire will give you 20 per cent?' Pradipta shot back.

'We won't be able to stand the sight,' Pakrashi smiled and walked away.

Pradipta had nothing to say. He did not care much about Bijoy, really. All he needed was his cheque in time and his packets of cigarettes. He wasn't particularly averse to Bijoy-babu also since he thought Bijoy was just another guy caught in the system. There was a faint trace of appreciation that Bijoy could be efficient in what he was doing, which was stealing for the owners, stalling, or doing nothing. Anyone who could forge a fraction of fifty thousand signatures alone must be competent in a peculiar way.

When Pradipta left the three-wheeler, it was caught in the usual rush outside the plant's Gate 9. Pradipta knew he could reach Majhi's home faster if he walked through Golchowk bazaar and cut across the park to reach the railway colony. This was a route he would never take after sundown when the park would be saturated with loving couples. But during the day, only a few plant workers would be sleeping in the shade of trees, their siesta at times jolted by the thud of rubber balls hit with gay abandon by children playing cricket.

Majhi worked from his home at the workers' quarters where he and his father had lived for the last forty years. His father was a railway engine driver, and after his death, plant union president Hari Trivedi proclaimed the house to be 'a symbol of workers' struggle'.

Majhi's father was never part of any struggle, though. He simply drove goods trains which ferried essential supplies to the plant, and drank his usual glasses of rum, topped with country liquor, when he came back from his frequent trips.

Before coming back home late in the night, he would spend an hour in the park. All the girls knew him so well that they would call him Pilot-dada. Once, Majhi had bumped into his father in the park. 'I thought you would be in Palasganj.'

'I thought you would be in Hirapur and not in the park,' Majhi's father shot back, as they walked out of the darkness together.

Majhi was almost broke, and his trip to Hirapur hadn't materialized because of that. Since he could claim reimbursement only after he came back from a trip, he did not go at all. He talked to the police superintendent in the town and filed his story on the massacre, datelined Hirapur.

It made a banner headline in the paper: 'Women, Children, Old Men Massacred in Hirapur. 27 Dead, 100 Injured, 3,000 Houses Burnt.'

'That's always the case. One does the work, the other takes the cake. In this case, the women in the park should have got the flat for nurturing the struggle,' said Pradipta.

'But then I would have to live in the park, and you would have to join me there since none of us would have got any pay cheques,' countered Majhi.

Pradipta hoped Bijoy would oblige. Even though Amal would underwrite his stay at the lodge indefinitely, Pradipta did not want to give Manager-babu the impression that he was a hack who never got paid.

'There is a real threat to Bijoy's dhoti,' thought Pradipta, as he walked underneath the culvert with a cigarette hung from his lips. He wouldn't light it till he reached Majhi's home or office or whatever. He needed the cigarette for the initial period of wait. He wasn't sure how well-stocked Majhi was.

As he turned the corner, he initially focused on the plant gate. There were a few people around the guard booth. They stood there with no purpose at all. Pradipta thought perhaps a minor agitation was taking shape, perhaps by contract labour. There was nothing unusual in it. Such protests were regularly held by the union with a nod from the management. This way, the union retained its control over workers, and the management retained its control over the union. Rather, the union bosses and the management retained their control over everybody else.

Pradipta recalled he was involved in organizing one such protest actually. He believed he was saving a job.

'It's not a question of saving a job, it was hoodwinking poor, desperate workers,' argued Amal.

'It's easy for you to theorize,' said Pradipta, 'since you don't have to deal with them. I used to write this guy's letters, and his wife was in the district hospital. She is probably dead now. Then it was a question of saving one life, one job and one family.'

'You sure you saved them?'

'Am sure I did the right thing. In any case, purely from a theoretical standpoint, it's better to fool workers than to let that bastard Parekh sack someone. And for what? For simply smoking a bidi on the shop floor?'

'Where do we stop justifying the means?' Amal pressed on.

'That is for theoreticians like you to figure out. For me, I couldn't let anyone get sacked. And why couldn't he smoke?'

'The plant would then be worse than Pinatubo.'

'The problem was not with smoke and ash. The bastard simply blew rings in Parekh's face.'

'I don't contest someone's right not to like passive smoking.'

'I don't like passive drinking either. Parekh stinks of liquor. If you can down a peg or two in your office room, I can very well finish half a reefer on the shop floor. An MD can have more pay and privileges but not more drinking and abusing rights. Fairness demands that the right to abuse must be equally distributed.'

'You can't run a plant unless you can bark,' Amal continued, realizing his case was weakening fast.

'You shouldn't then object when the other guy questions your ancestry.'

'It was a question of violation of plant rules.' Amal hung on.

'Right. But why isn't drinking in your office a violation of office rules simply because it is not stated in the standing orders?'

☙❧

Amal found standing his ground difficult since he was sliding into the realm of the indefensible. Like Pradipta, he felt Goshto's red-hot fish curry swirling in his stomach whenever Parekh's name came up. A soft red lump of liquid anger wound its way up inside, lodging in his throat, almost forcing him to spit out invectives. Parekh somehow always managed to disorient Amal. He would wrestle with the suave, shaved, after-shaved, rimless-spectacled creature that jumped out of the comic strip long lost in Amal's uncle's dust-covered attic. A shiny oval face and honeydew forehead turned Parekh into a weird cross between a Rishikesh sadhu and a sly antediluvian predator aimlessly loping across a lost forgotten world. Those who were stranded in his path would rue his neatly aligned enamel set that could easily chew chunks off their wages, if not eat up their jobs. A half-smile would lead to the cancellation of the day's overtime. A swift ear-to-ear grin was the harbinger of a one-week lay-off. The whiteness of the spread-out fangs stood out sharply against the blackness of the greased machines, reminding Parekh's subordinates that black was the colour of life.

As Pradipta turned the corner guarded by a gigantic black hill formed by slag and ash from the plant, a heap of gutted dreams of nameless furnace hands, he saw the crowd. The howling breeze grappled with hurricane heat in a dance of terminal madness, carrying minuscule fragments of plant rejects, depositing them on the panoply of steel and asphalt and human skin that formed life outside Gate 9.

Life now was frozen. The road could normally squeeze in five vehicles of various sorts in different directions. The constant honking by three-wheelers and cars, the incessant warnings shouted by indefatigable bus conductors clinging to window grilles, backed up periodically by brain-splitting electric horns, and the endless procession of men and cyclists wedged between vehicle headlamps and iron spikes trailing out of open trucks created the mirage of life in motion.

Life, however, was gone from the body of the young boy lying face up at the foot of the ash and slag hill. His eyes were open, hands outstretched, fingers bent as if he were making faces at his young sister who sat calmly nearby. He was dragged out of the slag heap by a plant security guard. It was not clear how the sister escaped the drowning in plant refuse.

Perhaps she was slow for once, a few steps behind her brother for some unknown reason. The boy always followed his elder sister quietly, wherever she went, whatever she did. He stuck to his sister like a shadow. But today he walked into the other world alone, leaving his sister behind.

It was she who was always up to something while the boy would even hesitate to get up and walk. She was thought to be a spoilt child by the teacher in the plant-operated free school. It was still not clear who had spoilt her.

Her mother earned just a few hundred rupees, washing clothes and dishes at officers' homes. She usually ate something at one of her employers' houses during the day. She feigned a lack of appetite at night when the children ate a few chapattis and some lentil or vegetables. The children always went to school where they could get a free meal during the day. A cup of milk, a boiled egg, and a long, soft, cheap bread that was common fare at teashops. It was tough when the school was closed or on weekends. Then food during the day was just a matter of luck.

But she didn't like studying. Whatever scraps of paper she brought to the shack from school she would fill with scribbles and drawings. She would keep drawing whenever she got a chance. Once, she drew a series of boats travelling upside down in a river where the sun had sunk to the riverbed.

'You will get a zero. Did you ever see a boat travelling upside down?' the teacher screamed.

ଓଃ

She had no answer. She never really had an answer to any of the things. She was dragged by her ear to the corner of the classroom, and then the teacher thought better of it and made her stand outside the classroom.

She was happy being the outcast. Unknowingly, she had begun to seek such punishment. Outside the room, there was a narrow corridor bound by a waist-high wall. The three classrooms were built one after another, on a line along the corridor. The school with just three rooms seemed to have begun abruptly from the middle of a wild bush and ended abruptly in the middle of another. The plant managers thought three classes would provide adequate educational skills to the children of migrant workers living in shacks on the edge of the golf course. She was in Class IV in one end, and her brother was in Class II at the other.

The school, in fact, fascinated the girl always. She would scramble up the hill at the foot of which the school was placed. It was hard to see it from a distance, even from a vantage point on the hill. It was hidden behind shrubs, a big *pipul* and a whole set of *palash*. In the months of May and June, when the land would turn into molten lava, the soil dissolving constantly into the ballast of heat, the crimson palash would set the school on fire. She would find freedom in the middle of the afternoon, take a long walk and climb up the hill. There was no food in the shack, but the walk kept her alive. Always the boy followed her, though not quite sure what she achieved.

'Why a headstand?' he wanted to know.

'Want to look at the school. If I stand here, the pipul is blocking my view. I want to go underneath the palash. Just hold my waist against the rock, will you?'

She stood on her head for a few minutes, slowly bent her knees, and came back to a normal position, smiling.

'When I look at you on my head, you look bigger.' She gave the boy a hard push, flinging him back against the loose, sandy soil. He jumped up in an instant, hurled himself back like a swaying banana tree in a raging monsoon, and grabbed her by the waist, and they both rolled together down the slope, screaming. Her shoulder hit the rock, and she laughed. He was always scared of her laughter since she could never stop.

The teacher had slapped her hard, splitting her lips, since she laughed while being thrown out of class.

'Show your teeth to your dad, you spoilt brat!' the teacher screamed maniacally.

The boy was scared of any talk of his father, whom he had never known or seen. But she never seemed to mind, never seemed to feel hurt about anything. She perhaps never had any time for anything, except to be thrown out of class, to run up the hill, and look underneath the palash, standing on her head. It was as if she was always in a hurry, rushing to fashion a different view of things around her, with boats floating upside down, a merciless heat burning her skin, a school which offered her various views from outside.

The boy never understood why the school looked different from various vantage points.

Once, it was raining at night, and the mother had sent word she would not be back before morning.

'Am going to school. The rain must be changing it somewhat now.'

They sat and lay on the muddy field across the corridor, with the water pounding their heads and back.

'It's so wonderful to be slapped.' She kept laughing.

The school was just a shadow from the distance, with a distant argon lamp posing as a low-hung shifting moon in the fierce night.

They ran to the school, and she touched the wall with her face, stretching her arms against the ashen wall as if she wanted to hold on to someone close to her. He sat on the corridor wall, watching a portion of her face illumined by the artificial moon.

'I believe all things can talk. You have to listen to them.'

'There is so much of noise around, how do you know?'

'You can if you are quiet. This is a lonely school. It needs us more than we need it.'

Someone had thought of the need for water and cleared a portion of the wild growth and sunk a tube well next to the third classroom. The tube well merged with the school on the canvas of a supreme artist. The three rooms and the tube well were inseparable. When the handle had broken, the school was closed for a few days. Finally, an iron handle was remodelled on a lathe to fit the contraption, and the school reopened with a gush of water.

She lay down under the faucet as the boy hung on to the handle, pulling it down and then jumping up. The rain was still pouring down, but the solid column of water cleansed her not just of the mud but all tiredness.

'Okay, you can go under now,' she offered.

'No, let's go. I have had a good bath.'

As Pradipta looked at the face, he first cursed himself. This was rare. He thought he should have given him one rupee, or even two, when he had clung to his hands. As if that rupee denied turned into a rupee conceded would change the indescribable feeling Pradipta had within him. It was not so much anger. Not so much pain or sorrow. It was more of a sickening feeling for himself. He didn't know why he was feeling that he could have changed the situation with one rupee. Perhaps it was a feeling of not doing enough.

'Shaala,' Pradipta said loudly, cursing himself. The crowd was swelling and generally silent, looking intently at the ashen face and then the quiet girl, and then generally at each other. Pradipta's loud curse woke them up. Since he was facing the general direction of the crowd where the plant's two security guards were also standing, the crowd assumed the 'shaala' was directed at the two men.

'*Maar saale ko*!' someone screamed. Within moments, the two plant men were within seconds of losing their lives. They tried to run away, rolled on the ground, and tried to get up and run again. One rolled near Pradipta's feet. Pradipta kicked him in the face, losing his right foot slipper in the process.

Again Pradipta was surprised at himself. He had never physically protested against any event. He had merely watched when the shanties were razed for the golf course.

He didn't even join the scuffle with the security guards and the police. His protests came out always in his writings, in the endless column centimetres he produced, in the numerous pages he designed, in the hundreds of letters and petitions he wrote for others. Even though he was not the rationalizing type like Amal, his anger had never been directed at security guards and others whom he considered to be as exploited as everyone else. Still, he kicked the man writhing on the ground in his face.

'Shaala,' he cursed himself again. Ash and dust had merged with screams and the sounds of shattering glass. A woman jumped out of a three-wheeler and first ran towards the plant gate and then towards Pradipta. She froze in front of the ashen body, bent down, and fell on top of him. With black tears smearing her face, she hugged the body as if trying to protect him from the chaos around. But no one paid any attention to the woman or the boy on her lap or his sister sitting in a trance next to them. The two guards were possibly dead, thought Pradipta, when the first tear-gas shell went up through the ash cloud and smoke from burning scooters and cars.

'Let's go!' Pradipta screamed at the woman with the body. She stared at Pradipta blankly.

A white mushroom cloud of tear gas was forming nearby. Pradipta could feel someone was trying to set his eyes alight with a cigarette lighter. The thought of attar and printer's ink flashed in his mind as he smelt the heady mixture of burning petrol and 2-chloro-benzal-malononitrile.

The woman next to him was, however, oblivious. She was still hugging the boy, and the girl was hugging the woman. Pradipta held the woman with one hand and seized the boy from her with the other and began to run. The girl followed.

Even in the thickness of the smoke and dust, Pradipta knew his way about. He could hardly open his burning eyes, but he knew he had to go for the Chowputty fence. That was his only refuge, like Manager-babu's mess. He must reach the enclosure before the next volley of tear gas. It was not that he thought about himself or was bothered about the searing pain that had turned his brain into minced meat. Somehow the thought of an unpaid rupee submerged all other physical and mental stimuli. The woman was hanging like a girl from one arm; the boy was hanging like a heavy rucksack from the other. The girl followed.

Chapter 5

The Chowputty fence was low, with gaping holes in various sections. He dragged the woman through a hole, heading for a tin shed that had been put up for no clear reason. It could have been done by some local boys who were making their presence known for some potential future claim. The park was sort of a no-man's land in a town that belonged to the plant. The plant never sent its security guards to the park, which was inhabited by different groups during the day and night. It was sort of a common heritage of all groups, an Antarctic with various claimants, a free zone with sleepers, players, strollers, drinkers, and activists going about their business without anyone walking over them. It was said even Parekh hadn't ever stepped into the park during the day.

Still, Pradipta's tin-shed target and the park refuge weren't too far removed from the muzzles launching shells in parabolic curves into the grey haze. As he dashed forward with his dead and alive companions on both hands towards the shed, he tripped over a partially standing brick wicket set up by boys the previous day and went head first into the ground. The boy flew into a strange cluster of marigold shrubs in the middle of nowhere, and the woman rolled on the ground on the other side. When he opened his eyes, he found himself lying on Majhi's veranda, with the woman sitting next to his head. The boy was lying on the floor, covered with a spotless white cloth, so white that it looked new. The grille gate was locked, with a mildly agitated crowd outside. Pradipta could hear Majhi shouting on the phone at someone. When he finally sat up, he was facing Amal leaning against the wall and the grille, looking at him intently.

'Did I really pass out?' Pradipta asked, ignoring the pain in his head and the molten eyes still reacting to traces of crowd-control chemicals.

Amal ignored him, opening the lock to let in the compounder who was more trusted than the doctor at the plant drugstore.

The compounder ignored Pradipta as well but grabbed him by the shoulder and turned his head around to reveal the black mess of dirt, blood, and ash above the temple on the left.

'Don't use raw Dettol,' Pradipta implored.

'Amal-babu, can you hold him from the back?' the compounder said and asked the woman to hand him a pair of scissors from his bag.

Amal grabbed Pradipta from behind, locking his arms around him more in the fashion of a friendly hug than a wrestler's grip. For once, it seemed to Amal, Pradipta didn't say anything or protest. He merely stared blankly at the boy lying next to him. He still had his eyes open and returned the frozen gaze. It was the second time Pradipta was knocked out by the force of beauty. The image of the woman who died when the shanties were razed covered his mind like a thin chiffon sari floating in the wind. Now the boy with a face covered with ash and grime and curly hair with bits of marigold petals stuck to it overwhelmed the woman's image. He didn't know which one was more beautiful or pure.

Pradipta grimaced as the woman cut off clumps of hair from the wound.

Pradipta's eyes were watery. He was grateful no one noticed that he was no longer coping with the after-effects of tearing chemicals.

Majhi had stopped yelling on the phone. Silence stalked the veranda as the compounder dressed Pradipta's wounds with the crowd peering through the screen of wrought iron lotuses and stems that formed the grille. The girl, Pradipta noticed her for the first time, watched quietly from a corner.

'I have to take the body, Pradipta-babu,' the officer-in-charge of the police station whispered. He could have howled through the mike fitted on the sunshade of the police van. It wouldn't have made as great an impact. The OC was the only man who seemed to have a voice, however feeble. Everyone else was quiet and motionless.

Pradipta did not respond.

'Pradipta-babu, are you all right?' asked the OC.

'How long will it take?' Amal asked.

'It should be over by late afternoon,' explained the OC.

'Even if a single hair of his is touched, I promise I will take you all apart,' Amal said softly, in a voice that no one had heard before. Pradipta looked at Amal who was looking at the OC. The OC turned his face, staring through the grille.

'Amal-babu, we have to do the post-mortem.'

'Do it on Parekh. I won't allow you to touch even his hair. Tell the doctor that. I don't care.' There was immovable madness in Amal's voice, which came from a distant world.

'I promise he won't be touched,' the OC said. 'We have to just go through certain formalities. You don't have to go anywhere. I will come with him after a couple of hours, and I am leaving behind one police jeep for your use. And maybe tomorrow I will have to speak to her,' the OC said, looking at the woman.

'You can only speak to her in my presence,' Amal said softly.

Pradipta hadn't noticed the woman did more of the cleaning and bandaging than the compounder. He looked into her eyes and asked her name.

'Chandni.'

'I am Pradipta, and this is Amal, this is - '

'Everyone knows you, babu.'

Twice in quick succession, Pradipta came face-to-face with dignity and madness. First it was Amal, who was speaking as if he would hate to wake the boy up lying next to him.

Then it was Chandni. She spoke so softly that in normal circumstances no one would have known she had spoken. Pradipta felt he was with strangers—he didn't know this Amal, and Chandni was too perfect to belong to his world of knowledge and rationality.

'We have to find a place for her, at least for the time being,' Amal said, putting his arms round Pradipta's shoulders.

'They can stay in the living room if they want. I don't have a problem,' said Majhi.

'Chandni, we will get your stuff later, and you are staying here,' Pradipta decided.

Chandni kept her head bowed, looking at her feet.

The OC left with the body.

☙❧

Pradipta felt relieved that the short acerbic Dr Avinash, who was perennially drunk, would be in charge. Pradipta and Amal knew him well and knew the place too.

It was called Kata Pukur, a pond that had been dug up. There was simply no pond around, and the structure that functioned as a morgue and post-mortem facility was placed in the middle of virtually nowhere. A dusty crimson unpaved lane ended at the foot of the metal gates, one part of which was partially unhinged from the concrete pillar to which it was fixed. There were no locks on the gates, and it was clear no one had attempted to close them for a long time since the metal was rusty and both sections were firmly stuck in the ground. The place was usually quiet, forlorn. Even the man entrusted with slashing and cutting human bodies would hardly utter a word. He would sit in the front room behind a thick wire mesh with a hole at about desk height. Pieces of paper would be thrust at him through the hole. He would examine the bits carefully, motion his couple of assistants, and vanish into an antechamber. This was a good sign for the people carrying a body in. It meant he would take a sip from a bottle of rum and cut up the body immediately, or maybe just write a report. Even though he was always drunk, no one could sway him.

Dr Avinash was a master of himself. If he didn't like something with the documents or had a problem with the entourage, he would walk off. The body would be left to rot or be eaten by rats. And since he doubled up as the man who cleared a body for cremation, his signature was vital for the well-being of people alive. The crematorium was dead for a long time for lack of electricity. Still, a clearance was needed for the body to be taken to the riverbank and burnt on a pyre. People were in awe of Dr Avinash and believed he was incorruptible.

For some reason, Dr Avinash liked the OC. Or, perhaps the OC found in Dr Avinash a harmless rum partner. On many evenings, the two could be seen immersed in a conversation in the light of a lantern, the half-empty rum glasses becoming shadowy blast furnaces on the bare whitewashed wall behind the duo as the periodic wind barged in, flinging aside a heavy jute curtain at the open door. No one in their right mind would ever step near the edifice. Even the police jeep would be parked some distance from Dr Avinash's two-room hutment, which was the nearest dwelling unit about half a kilometre from the morgue. The rest of the habitation was a long way off as if the whole town would rather not deal with the doctor of the dead. But it was the doctor who had a greater influence in the town than Parekh.

Parasin Dhobi was sitting on the pavement outside Gate 9, on the eve of a public holiday. Though it was still early in the evening, with the last rays of the orange globe setting alight the fiery palash at the foothills, Parasin couldn't care less. She had earned extra ten bucks for her cleaning job at the canteen, walked straight to the man with an earthen pitcher on the field near the gate, and paid for three glasses of greyish country liquor made from fermented rice.

Pradipta believed Chuni Lal needed a marketing man to turn him into the finest drinks manufacturer in the world.

'Chuni's stuff is better than vodka any day,' Pradipta pointed out. 'He just doesn't have a name.'

'Call it Ganga,' encouraged Amal.

'Not possible in this country. That would lead to riots. Maybe Brahmaputra. Barkatoki's son is Brahmaputra.'

'Perhaps Hooghly. It sounds like googly in the land of cricket,' said Amal, though he never knew how the liquor tasted.

Amal would stay well within the confines of rum or, if possible, gin. But Pradipta was a free spirit. If he was passing by, he would sit down in the field with Chuni, share a glass with him, and discuss plant politics. And on days Parasin joined the group, he would later follow Parasin to her hutment and down some *chhatu*, flour of roasted gram, with country liquor and lots of chillies and onions.

Parasin hadn't even seen that Parekh had pulled up where she was sitting. She was humming a film song;

There's a river in my village Hashiphari

Where we met under the palash tree

The earth's scorched dark brown

The boat's gone a long while without me

She had just taken a gulp of 'better than vodka' and faced up to find Parekh facing down.

Half the liquor in her mouth squirted out, wetting Parekh's trousers.

Parekh let flow a string of expletives. A couple of plant guards ran in, picking up Parasin by her hair and an arm.

'Don't ever step into the plant again!' screamed Parekh.

'Don't ever pee into your trousers,' replied Parasin, as she was dragged away.

Parasin went straight to Dr Avinash. She was one of the few who could venture out there. She would go there once or twice a week to clean up. There was not much cleaning needed, really. Dr Avinash had just a few clothes, which he would wash and dry himself; a large kit bag stuffed with some books, papers, and clothes; a few glasses, plates, utensils, and bottles; a cot with a mattress; and a black-and-white fourteen-inch TV. The TV was very old, and the picture was fuzzy, though the sound was crystal clear. Still, Parasin would sweep the floor with total devotion, clean the dishes, arrange the items, and if on rare occasions there was some electricity flowing in, in the evening, she would switch on the TV and watch the dramas. She had an absolute run of the place since Dr Avinash hardly ever spoke. He would sit at the desk near the cot and drink rum alone, unless of course he was joined by the OC. Parasin would stay at her corner on the ground.

'He abused me and his thugs molested me,' said Parasin, by this time much less drunk, with tears welling up at the corner of her eyes. 'What will I do, Doctor-babu?'

'Did he say you can't go in tomorrow?' asked Dr Avinash, not waiting for an answer, leaving his glass for once and walking slowly to the rotary phone kept on the windowsill.

'Parekh, I want you to say sorry publicly to Parasin tomorrow and raise her pay by ten bucks,' said Dr Avinash matter-of-factly. 'Or else I will fix you and your guards with an 'attempt to rape' charge.' Dr Avinash put down the phone. There was the same precision in his voice as he always displayed while cutting up corpses.

Parasin was crouching down at the feet of Dr Avinash, weeping softly. Dr Avinash touched her shoulders and slowly picked her up.

'There's some warm water still in the bucket. Go and have a wash.'

When Parasin came back, the OC was at the table.

'Did they touch you?' asked the OC.

Parasin kept quiet.

Dr Avinash poured a little rum into a glass and some water and handed it to Parasin.

'It's all right. It might not be as good as the stuff you have every day, but it should do,' said Dr Avinash.

'Can you get us some Chuni's chullu tomorrow?' asked the OC.

Parasin looked at Dr Avinash. For once, there was a flicker of a smile on Dr Avinash's face, though Parasin couldn't say for certain in the lantern light.

'Yes, you must get us some of Chuni's magic,' said Dr Avinash, handing over a tenner to Parasin.

'I will get it free, babu. I will just tell him it's for you.'

'No, I will have it free when I go there one day.' Parasin took the note, knowing Dr Avinash hadn't gone anywhere apart from the morgue.

Parekh gathered a crowd at the canteen.

'I am sorry, Parasin. Please forgive me if I had offended you in any way,' said Parekh.

Parasin kept quiet, threw her hair back, and walked away.

ଔ

The OC carried the boy himself to the morgue. He parked his jeep as he usually did at a distance from Dr Avinash's rooms and then walked to the morgue. The boy seemed asleep in his arms.

Dr Avinash walked out from behind his mesh. No one could remember when he had ever done that.

'Went under the slag heap at the main gate,' said the OC.

'Where was he all this while? It must have happened at least a few hours ago,' asked Dr Avinash.

'Yes, there was firing. Pradipta-babu took the boy and her mother to Majhi's place. Amal-babu says you can't touch him,' said the OC.

'Where is Pradipta-babu? Amal-babu?'

'He was hit in the head. He passed out for a while.'

Dr Avinash went back behind the desk, opened the drawer, and took out a fifty-rupee note. He spoke to one assistant, 'Take the bike and get a pair of shorts and a shirt. Get two sizes and tell them I need them. I will return the one that doesn't fit.'

He turned to the OC. 'I won't touch him, but he must be dressed up because he is going to heaven.'

Pouring rum into a glass and an earthen cup, he gave the glass to the OC and took the cup himself. They did not speak. The boy was lying on the concrete slab beyond the wire mesh. The afternoon sun that peeked through the broken skylight played gently with the boy's hair and face. The distant humming of a water pump added to the silence of the room. As the assistant arrived with a floral shirt and grey shorts, Dr Avinash walked behind the mesh and took out a white plastic bottle containing formalin. He poured a bit of the liquid on a wad of cotton and wiped a portion of the concrete slab with it. The assistant walked away, unable to endure the burning in his eyes. The OC put on dark glasses, hoping the formalin fumes would not dissolve his eyeballs.

Dr Avinash did not seem to be affected. He dressed the boy in a blue and white floral shirt and grey shorts, hugged him gently, and carried him to the OC. He signed a couple of papers and gave them to the OC. As the OC carried the boy to the jeep, Dr Avinash went back to his earthen cup and sat down. No words were spoken.

ଓଃ୬ଚ

Chapter 6

Pradipta had just turned his head towards the beginning of the lane as the jeep turned the corner. A few people were hovering outside the veranda as if someone special was about to make an appearance. They all moved aside as the OC, carrying the boy in his arms, walked in. The sunlight was getting diffused, and the declining afternoon heat flowed as a soothing balm through all the bodies assembled on the tiny veranda. Chandni was at the corner on the ground, on her haunches, with her chin resting on her palm, looking down. The girl was leaning against her, peering through the grille, following the frolics of two sparrows on a *bakul* tree across the lane. Pradipta stood leaning against the wall, next to Chandni, staring straight ahead. Amal sat on the veranda stairs, with a portion of the body supported by the corner of the wall. The only person who was on a round plastic chair was Majhi, with his legs stretched out in a way as if he had forbidden anyone from crossing to the other side.

The OC stepped over Majhi's legs as he carried the body in. Pradipta very slowly walked into the room and pulled out a bed linen and lay it on the ground. Even after the OC had put the boy down where the linen had been placed, no one spoke. No one was in any hurry to do anything, as if it were one of those lazy days of a general strike when nothing moved.

Parasin was the first to speak from the lane.

'Babu, I have got these palash flowers for our child,' she said, looking at Amal.

Amal stood up, held Parasin by her hand, and brought her in. She placed the flowers on the boy's chest. The red palash swam effortlessly with the white gardenias in the blue ocean on the shirt.

'Amal-babu, you can take the jeep,' the OC pleaded.

'Thanks. We would walk.' Amal spoke so softly he could hardly be heard, but his voice had the sharpness of Dr Avinash's knife sinking into naked flesh. As Amal picked up the boy, the OC stepped aside to make way. Pradipta reached out to Chandni, held her around the shoulders, and pulled her up. The girl followed her mother as everyone stepped onto the dusty unpaved lane leading to nowhere.

Amal was carrying the boy in his arms as if he were asleep. He did not take the usual route which led to the township, but turned the other way. The winding lane had merged into an unkempt field and wilderness. But there was a shortcut through the shrubs and vegetation to the river which not many people knew. Parasin, of course, knew the lay of the forested area like the back of her hand since she spent most of her evenings there, singing, dancing and drinking country liquor supplied free to her by Chuni Lal.

'Parasin, can you go up in front?' Amal requested.

Parasin ran ahead, as if she were leading a victory march, humming a tune. She quickly led to a track that at times went in different directions. But Parasin was undeterred, happily walking, jumping across fallen branches blocking her way. The silent marchers were trailed by the girl, who was always a few steps behind the entourage, her progress being slowed down by unusual sightings of birds, insects and foliage.

The path took a sharp turn and dropped into the river. If one was not careful, one could easily walk into the river in the evening. The single-file procession walked on the edge to reach a clearing where the river had veered off for about a couple of dozen feet. The whitish sand was tarnished with blackened evidence of burnt-out funeral pyres. No fires were burning this evening, and apart from Amal and his group, there was not even a soul around. Parasin vanished into the forested area in descending darkness and soon emerged with a drunken young man who promised to carry out the proceedings for just a few rupees. Parasin reached an agreement, and the man again went into the forest and came back with another man, carrying firewood, dry branches, and a jerrican of kerosene.

Pradipta lit the pyre as the ochre sun hung low across the river. The drunken man mumbled, 'Om, Bhur Bhuva Swaha . . .' before Amal softly asked him to shut up. The fire assumed its destructive form, rising in cleansing rage, matching the ferocity of the river. The roar of the swirling waters and the howling forest wind enthused the dancing flames soaring high into the evening sky. The tribal drums began to sound deep inside the forest, adding to the music of the universe. Still there was a strange silence amid the lunacy of light and sound.

Chandni stared blankly at the untamed fire, with the girl leaning against her. Pradipta sat motionless at the foot of a large pupil tree. From a distance, in the enveloping darkness, it seemed he was in meditation. He was a couple of body lengths behind Chandni, but he was not looking at the fire or anyone. He seemed to be seeing through Chandni and following the mad rush of the river in spate. Pradipta merely turned a couple of pebbles in his hand from time to time as Parasin, the drunken man, and his pupil tended the fire.

They were the absolute masters of burning bodies. The second man would walk up to the pyre and poke it with a long stick. The drunken man would walk steadily with his jerrican and hurl some fluid on portions where the fire was being subdued by the wind. Parasin dragged a half-torn car tyre from inside the forest and pushed it inside the pyre where the flame refused to live. The smell of burning rubber and kerosene merged with the intoxicating *mohua* wafting in from the tribal gathering in the darkness. It was a combat between wind and fire, with the former wrestling to pin the fire down as it inevitably broke free, leaping high into the blackness.

No one had noticed Pradipta walking into the forest. When he came out, he was holding another jerrican and a few earthen cups. He walked up to Amal and poured the liquid. Amal, who had never touched the local stuff before, did not refuse. Pradipta offered some to Chandni, who simply nodded her head. But as the girl looked up to Pradipta, he poured a little bit of the liquid in the cup and gave it to her. Amal looked at Pradipta and the girl. She waited for a while as if she expected Amal to say something, and then she gulped the liquid in one movement and leaned against Chandni. Pradipta filled his cup to the brim, and left the jerrican with Parasin and the two men.

When the fire finally gave up its struggle with the wind, it was well into the night. Pradipta took the jerrican with *mohua*. There was still a little bit of the liquid left, which he poured on the last few embers. He then walked towards the river.

'Babu, careful!' screamed Parasin, in the stillness of the night, as she ran and snatched the jerrican from Pradipta's hands. The drunken man had also come running. Parasin held the jerrican with the right hand as Pradipta held her left hand. The drunken man held Pradipta around the waist. The three-member human chain moved one step at a time towards the river. Parasin bent low, stretched her hand, and let the waters crash against the container.

Pradipta poured the water on the remains, soothing the last vestiges of life.

As the human forms made their way back, Parasin was again in the lead. They walked in a single file on the edge, with everyone holding on to the other's hand. Even with the eyes getting used to the darkness, one could only pierce the unknown for just a couple of feet. Every step seemed like a final push into the embrace of an irresistible force.

Parasin, fearless and nonchalant, hummed:

Take me to the other side
Where the moon floats
The palash lights her face
Stars merged in the evening tide

Where love wafts through foliage
As she waits
Like eternity in unbound space
Oh! Take me once
Take me to the other side

ঌ

Chapter 7

If you need it, it's on the lentil
Pink molten wax, blackened wick
Surviving the rainy night before

If you want, it's on the bookshelf
A few pages turned inside
The terracotta spine curved from load unknown
If you believe, it's in the darkness
Invading the corners
The golden Buddha stands with hands outstretched

Pradipta repeated the lines as he pushed open Majhi's grill gates. Before Majhi could get up, Chandni came out with a round chair whose seat and back were made of blue and white plastic straps. It was Pradipta's place of refuge, as he leaned back, stretching his legs, to light his third cigarette of the day. It wasn't morning as such even though the plant's first shift had started. There was a bit of smoke and haze, especially in the veranda where smoke from the coal stove lit by Chandni had settled in the corners.

Pradipta had once asked if Chandni could work with a gas oven. She nodded her head in disagreement, and since then, she would get up at the break of dawn to light the coal fire. By the time Pradipta stepped in, the smoke would clear. It wasn't that Pradipta cared too much about smoke. He only thought a gas oven could have been easier to handle.

Chandni came in with two earthen cups of tea and cookies from the tea stall at the bend in the road. There were five ceramic cups with blue *rajanigandha* etched on them in the house. But both Pradipta and Majhi preferred the earthen cups. The ceramic was used by Chandni and the girl. As Chandni bent down to place the cups on the plastic strip woven table, her hand touched Pradipta's.

Pradipta looked up. 'Since when are you having a fever?'

Chandni walked away, stepping into the room. Pradipta followed quickly, seizing her hand. Chandni did not say a word. Her hand was as hot as the teacup; her face was purplish brown in the soft light.

Pradipta let go, walking towards the black rotary phone in the corner.

'Is it working?'

'I hope so,' said Majhi, who was standing at the front door. Chandni hadn't left the room. She was standing at the other door, leaning against the frame, with her face turned away from Pradipta's and Majhi's, and half covered by the door curtain.

'It seems Chandni's seriously ill,' Pradipta informed Dr Avinash. 'I can take her to you if you want.'

No one had ever seen Dr Avinash leave the morgue. He also never treated anyone. Once Chuni Lal had a deep gash on his right leg after a night in the forest and had passed out. He was taken to Dr Avinash since he was taken to be dead. Dr Avinash stitched his wound and revived him. There was no other instance when he had seen anyone in the town.

'Thanks,' Pradipta said, hanging up.

Dr Avinash came within a few minutes on a scooter that was not his. Even though he didn't have anything of his own, people knew he could get anything in the town.

Chandni was sitting in the corner; the girl who had quietly come in was sitting at the other end. Without even glancing at Chandni, Dr Avinash asked the girl, 'When did this happen?'

'For the last two days, sir. She hasn't eaten anything.'

As Dr Avinash walked towards Chandni, he asked if Pradipta could rush a blood sample to the plant clinic.

'Tell them I want a report now and I don't care if they are open or closed or whatever. Give me the phone if anyone makes a fuss,' said Dr Avinash, as he sat down beside Chandni, feeling her pulse. Chandni leaned against Dr Avinash as if she wanted to embrace him. Dr Avinash put his arms round Chandni's shoulders and held her firmly, while Pradipta and Majhi lifted her from the floor and took her to Majhi's room and placed her on the bed.

The room was clean since there was not much in it anyway. A wooden wardrobe was placed at a corner, on top of which was a suitcase with a khaki gabardine covering with brown buttons in front. There was a jute bag, fronted by a dark-blue face of Goddess Kali, filled with papers, gathering dust. There were two wooden chairs flaunting floral patterns. One had lily-like flowers climbing upwards at the back. The other had interconnected petals, a couple of which had fallen off. The furniture was quickly rearranged on Dr Avinash's instructions.

The suitcase with gabardine prophylaxis was placed on the floor on top of which the lily-patterned chair was ensconced to give it more height. The cupboard was pushed to the side of the bed, and a brick was placed on top of it. A nylon string, tied to the brick and the chair, formed the line from which medicinal bottles would hang perilously.

Dr Avinash scribbled furiously in the girl's exercise book. Pradipta tore off the two pages, took the blood sample, and sped off in Dr Avinash's Vespa.

'She has slipped into a coma,' said Dr Avinash, as Amal walked in.

'How bad is it?' asked Amal, as he sat down at the head of the bed placing a cloth soaked in water on Chandni's forehead.

'Can't say,' said Dr Avinash, putting down the phone. 'We need to give her intravenous quinine right now. Every second could be crucial.'

The mercury had shot through the thin glass tube, but still Dr Avinash kept taking the temperature every few minutes. It was evening when for the first time Dr Avinash left Chandni's room where glasses and bottles filled with rum and *mohua* had been arranged.

'I am in love with *mohua* tonight,' said Pradipta, surprising everyone since there had been hardly a word spoken since morning. Dr Avinash picked up an earthen cup filled to the brim with rum, as Amal walked in to pick up his share of the liquid offerings.

'She can't be left alone even for a second,' said Dr Avinash.

'Babu, you stay here, I will be inside,' said Parasin, before anyone could react.

Majhi knelt down in front of Dr Avinash. 'Should we shift her to the plant hospital?' Dr Avinash looked at him intently for a while and then looked away.

The girl had fallen off to sleep, with her head on the bed next to her mother. Pradipta carried her gently in his arms and laid her down on the other wooden bed in the alcove next to the kitchen, which was shared by the mother and daughter. 'Will Mother die?' she asked, as Pradipta covered her with Majhi's shawl.

'Not even God can take her,' said Pradipta, running his fingers through the girl's hair as she closed her eyes again.

The dawn must have stepped in softly since no one had noticed the light creeping in. Only Parasin's tray full of *cha* led to stirrings in the room.

'May I have cha, babu?' Chandni had asked so softly that it seemed like a voice from the other world.

Dr Avinash was the first to react, hugging Chandni on the bed. 'Yes, we have won,' he announced.

Majhi and Amal propped up Chandni to a reclining position on the bed with pillows. Pradipta was holding on to her hand into which ran the intravenous drip.

❧

It had been almost a year since the boy died, but Chandni had hardly spoken a word since then. She would cook for everyone in the house, which usually meant Majhi, Pradipta, the girl, and herself, and at times, Amal. Pradipta had stopped eating at the mess, and even Amal at times skipped meals there, which Manager-babu didn't like. But Amal had the kind of stature at the lodge which no other residents ever enjoyed. Manager-babu had even asked Amal to stay in the room free, fearing that Amal might leave one day. Pradipta would stay most nights at the lodge but would, at times, sleep on the floor in the front room of Majhi's if it had been raining or if it was too late.

Apart from cooking, Chandni still worked during the day at a couple of plant homes. Pradipta had barred her from working on weekends. She listened to what the men told her to do, but she quietly ruled in the house. If Majhi had a shirt with a button missing, she would stitch it up without anyone knowing. If Pradipta smoked too many cigarettes, she just appeared at the door, and Pradipta would stamp out a newly-lit stick. Months had flown by without anyone realizing what Chandni needed till she collapsed in a coma. It was not that the men were insensitive. It was just that Chandni never spoke, and she absolutely needed nothing. Once Pradipta bought two handloom saris for Chandni. She wore them during the Pujas.

Amal supported Chandni's head with his one hand and with the other was holding the teacup for Chandni. She was drinking from it very slowly.

Pradipta held on to the needle-pierced hand.

'You are not going to leave me ever,' said Pradipta, staring intently at Chandni.

Chandni did not respond but gripped Pradipta's hand a little more firmly perhaps, with a distant look fixed on the *shimul* visible through the window. No one moved in the room for several minutes, forming a freeze-frame from a 1960s black-and-white film. The girl, by this time, had woken up and, without fuss, had occupied a corner of the room, lying on her stomach on the floor, with one chin propped up with one hand and the other gripping a broken inch-sized brown crayon. A half-torn sheet of paper with a half-finished flying boat had flown to a distance from where the girl was lying. She did not make any attempt to retrieve it, simply content with staring at the page wrapped around the leg of the bed.

Amal had his back to the inmates, leaning on his elbows on the windowsill. Dr Avinash was sitting on the floor, leaning against the cupboard, with a half-filled earthen cup of tea already cold. Parasin leant against the door frame, hair unkempt and with eyes red, partly from *mohua,* partly from sleeplessness, and partly from a few tears, which had rolled down her cheeks and dried up, unnoticed by all especially her. Majhi sat with his back to the wall, legs stretched, and looked vacantly at Chandni and the crowd in front. Pradipta was still holding on to her hand, head tilted to the right, shifting his gaze from the semi-comatose woman to the floor. No one smoked in the room. Strangely, no one felt the need to smoke.

Dr Avinash was the one to make the first move. 'She will need a long time to recover.'

A film song wafted in from distant shores, reminding the night-stayers it was the morning of Saraswati Puja.

Where's the unvanquished blue flower

Appearing in the morning

Where's the forgetful strummer

Haunting a restless forest night

Where's the awkwardly sloping path

Delving deep into the lake

There I wait for your footsteps

Along with shadows and the ruffling wind

ଔ

Chapter 8

Right at the corner of the grilled veranda was a kadam tree, and across the unpaved dusty lane, diagonally opposite, was a *krishnachura*. Both stood steadfast as wooden pylons guarding the few houses which seemed dispersed by a supreme planner from the main clusters of buildings in the town. Majhi's was at the end of the lane leading to nowhere, a vast wilderness of shrubbery and odd clumps of *jarul, pipul,* and *shimul*. Jackals roamed freely at night, calling out from the darkness.

At the other end of the lane that merged into a barren field was Haridev's cow pen, fenced by an exposed brick wall. Parts of the brickwork had been dislodged in two places, forming a hole through which goats, dogs and hens made their forays and a narrow passageway that was dominated by cows. A rusted metal gate clung to a single hinge, leaving a space wide enough for a bulky car to squeeze through, which looked more like a boat swept ashore by a gigantic wave in ancient times. The car, partly hidden in the undergrowth, was now a metal shell shorn of its wheels and an abode of dogs in the summer heat.

As Chandni came out through the gate with an aluminium can of milk, the girl was already standing on the footboard of the scooter with Pradipta firmly in the saddle. Chandni looked Pradipta's way.

'Will come back and have tea,' Pradipta explained.

Chandni stared at the cloud of dust scooped up by the scooter as if the two were leaving on a long journey.

It was not long before Pradipta came back alone, which was a good sign since it meant the girl was in school. Most days she wouldn't go to school, preferring to meander through the dusty lanes or making her coloured boats float upside down in black, blue and green rivers. It was a free school with the attendance rising and falling like the boats on loose sheets of paper.

'Where does our river go?' she had asked.

'To the ocean,' Pradipta explained.

'Where is the ocean?'

'Far away.'

'Will you take me there one day?'

'Maybe. But now you must read.' Pradipta tried to put a stop to the line of questioning.

It was not usually difficult to do so. The questioning would stop, but the boats would keep coming in endless shapes and colours. Mostly it was crayons that she used and, at times, watercolours. The large majority was made of HB pencils of different thicknesses and lengths. The room was wallpapered with pencilled boats, crayoned rivers and watercoloured expanse and sky. The last crayons were supplied by Amal, which were devoured in exactly two days. Once when she ran out of pencils and colour, she dipped her fingers in the mud and created a muddy river on the wall.

As Pradipta drowned in the rivers on the wall, Chandni brought tea in the ceramic cup covered by a stainless-steel plate. As she placed the cup on the floor next to Pradipta, he looked at her intently.

'Where's yours?'

Chandni left the room and came back with another cup—another *rajanigandha* with a chipped rim—and a plate of fried onions.

Pradipta kept looking at the plate. It was an unusual offering. He knew that Chandni knew he had cha always in earthen cups. And there had never been fried onions in the mornings. Chandni sat on the floor with her back to the wall, looking at her feet. Pradipta was lost in Chandni. When Amal came in, the plate of fried onions was untouched. Amal dipped into it, without saying a word. The three seemed to be floating in a river of tranquillity—for how long no one knew. The trance was broken by the unhurried chugging of the scooter that halted outside the veranda. As Dr Avinash and Majhi stepped in, along with the girl, Chandni left the room.

'I had thought at least today she would finish school,' Pradipta said to no one in particular.

'If I could come here, there was little sense of leaving her behind,' Dr Avinash said to no one in particular.

As Chandni walked in with more cha, Pradipta put the unlit cigarette back in the pack.

Before she could again leave, Dr Avinash put his arm round her shoulders, guiding her back to the centre of the room.

'I have come here only for you, and I will keep coming,' said Dr Avinash. 'No one here knows today is your birthday, except me. But all can forget to die, yet never forget this day again.'

As Chandni looked down with the eyes glistening at the corners, the girl ran in and clung on to her around the waist. Majhi opened a small paper bag made from discarded newspapers, handing out biscuits to all. Before Chandni, still looking down, could eat her share of the cookie, Pradipta grabbed her hand, took the piece from her, and put it in her mouth. Chandni did not resist.

Parasin had entered the room unnoticed. She took out a greenish glass bottle in which kerosene was usually stored and poured out the contents that looked like kerosene into the cups on the plastic-strip table.

'Chuni Lal's best country liquor, babu,' Parasin assured before anyone could object.

'To Chandni,' said Dr Avinash, raising his earthen cup.

'To Chandni,' said Amal.

Pradipta mixed the remaining portion of the tea left in a cup with the kerosene-lookalike liquor, raised the cup towards Chandni, and drank the liquid in one gulp.

'It burns better than kerosene,' said Pradipta.

Majhi gave more biscuits to the girl as Parasin drank from the bottle.

The only person who was not drinking or eating was Chandni, who looked sideways at Pradipta, not looking down for the first time.

'I want to live with you, Chandni, you are the reason for my existence,' said Pradipta.

The quiet flow of the fiery brew in the room was backed up by Dr Avinash's soft humming;

There never was a promise
A long list of succulent phrases
There wasn't any black ink
Under the glare of many gazes

There was no future
With death shorn of graces
Only a look, a momentary touch
As time stops in paces

ঔ

Chapter 9

The early light hadn't seeped through the broken windowpane partially covered with the torn front page of *The Murigram Post*. A bit of the tribal leader Sitaram Munda's face swayed in the December wind that rushed in through the corners. The girl was curled up under the blanket against the wall, striving in her sleep to hide from the freezing breeze.

Pradipta tried a similar response against the opposite wall, still in his sweater and trousers, which he would hardly get out of. Chandni wrapped herself all over with the black shawl as she walked quietly to the kitchen to find a way to deal with the unrelenting wind. She was overcautious not to disturb the rare morning silence. It was one of those rare days when all those who died inch by inch for *The Murigram Post* would get a few hours' rest.

But time away from office had been indeed rare since they launched *The Murigram Post* months ago in the town. Amal and Pradipta left the lodge after assuring Manager-babu they would keep going back and rented a room near the office along with Ranen and Pagla. Pradipta had of course another place to turn to–Majhi's flat where he shared a room with Chandni and the girl.

The previous night was more tense and threatening than usual. Chandni was not sure what had actually happened. It must have been around eight in the evening when the tea boy from Banshi's shop ran into the smoke-filled newsroom.

'Dadababu, they are killing Pagla-dada,' cried the boy.

Amal was the first to react. From where he was sitting, the only way he could quickly make his way to the door was over the desk. He basically rolled over the desk, spilling and dispersing everything that lay in his way from subbed copy to cups, as he dived through the door. Pradipta did exactly the opposite, sliding under the desk from his chair and exiting the other side. Even Ranen, who would usually be excited by matters concerning the other sex, ran towards the door. Chandni ran across the press floor, clambered over the low brick wall, and ran out to Banshi's shop without uttering a word.

Pagla lay on the dirt road, with Chandni huddled over Pagla, protecting him from the ongoing kicks and slaps. Amal's shirt, smeared in blood, was in half, hanging from his right shoulder. Pradipta kicked someone, who screaming, cursing, rushed in with a soda-water glass bottle from Banshi's shop, going straight for Pradipta's head.

The bottle made a loud thud as it landed on Banshi's left shoulder, spraying a fair amount of red fluid on Pradipta's face and down Banshi's back.

ঞ্চ

Banshi was a burly, pitch-dark character, with a shiny forehead that merged with the smooth bald patch covering the top of his head. Two clumps of glistening dark hair were equally distributed between his two temples, giving him the demeanour of a TV presenter on a late-night current affairs show. He looked ominous at six feet four when he stood up, which he rarely did since he was only seen huddled over two wooden boxes with glass fronts full of paan, cigarettes, and a few lozenges, chocolates, and home-made cookies from early morning till late night.

Amal was quite certain Banshi was a yogi in his last life.

'He sits motionless making those paans. If I could sit like that for eighteen hours every day, I would find God,' said Amal.

This was one subject where Pradipta usually agreed with Amal, or most of them did.

'How do you know he hasn't?' said Pradipta, to keep the conversation going.

'He must be having a PhD in neuroscience,' said Pagla.

'Possible. That's easier to get than getting God,' said Amal.

For Pradipta, Banshi was certainly a saviour, or more precisely, his shoulder was, as it took the brunt of the soda bottle blow. The attacker stood motionless for a couple of seconds, trying to comprehend the consequences of his action. Banshi caught his right hand, yanking it behind his back. The man fell to the ground screaming. Pradipta picked him up by his collar, dragging him towards the nullah that ran between Banshi's shop and the office gate.

The headlights of the police jeeps worked as fast-moving strobe lights on a dance floor, illuminating the crowd as the vehicles approached the melee on the undulating terrain. By the time the jeeps came to a halt and police superintendent Anil Singh stepped out, those who had started it all had vanished into the darkness. Chandni held Pagla around his shoulders as he sat on the dirt road.

'You could file an FIR here,' said Anil Singh, as he approached Amal.

'I will go to your office,' said Amal.

'You have to be careful with these guys, they are from the streets,' said Anil Singh.

No one replied.

Banshi, by this time, was sitting down on the road, with Chandni attending to his wound.

ఔ

Fifteen-year-old Jishu, who worked as Banshi's assistant, ran in with a lighted Petromax, furiously pumping in air. The mantle turned incandescent white, mirroring the quiet rage of Amal and others.

'I should be able to get hold of one or two of them soon,' said Anil Singh, looking at Amal.

Amal looked at Banshi, bending to see how deep the wound was.

'You need a tet-vax and some stitches,' said Dr Avinash, who had just walked in unnoticed. No one knew how Dr Avinash had got wind of the clash or who informed him.

A wooden bench, which was two wooden planks nailed together on top of four short bamboo sticks, was placed in front of Dr Avinash. Another Petromax was hung by Pradipta from a rope tied to the office gate and Banshi's wooden-tin shack. It hung directly above Banshi's head, who sat on the bench. Dr Avinash handed a roll of cotton from his shoulder bag to Chandni, who quickly poured Mercurochrome from a bottle on a swab and started cleaning the wound. Dr Avinash, his face just inches from Banshi's shoulder, inspected the injury for what seemed like eternity before he started stitching up the cuts. Chandni sat next to Banshi, holding on to his right hand firmly, while the girl carried an aluminium plate on her head, with earthen cups of tea on it and Amal following him.

'I will post two armed constables at the gate round the

clock,' Anil Singh said generally, as if he were talking to himself, walking towards his jeep.

No one looked his way.

ശ്ര

Banshi's shoulder was heavily bandaged by Chandni under Dr Avinash's gaze and instructions. She also fixed Pagla's broken spectacles with a white string, giving functionality back to Pagla. Strangely, the glasses had survived the fall and the pounding, but the frame hadn't. One stick had broken into two, and the right eyeglass had just come off intact and got stuck onto the side of the nullah, where it was discovered by the girl. Pradipta lay on the ground face down and stretched his right hand, carefully extracting the oval piece that looked like a soda-bottle bottom in its thickness and opacity.

Pagla was blind without his specs. He always went to sleep wearing his glasses, lying on his back, surveying the ceiling.

'Minus ten in both eyes,' Pagla had said.

No one knew if Pagla was accurate in his power projections, but it didn't really matter since whatever Pagla said was usually accepted as true. He said little, but it was understood he wouldn't waste his energy cooking up a tale.

'If you are minus ten, you couldn't have caught the blooper in the caption proof that was eight points and smudged,' Pradipta continued the discourse.

'I wasn't minus ten to begin with, my dad was, and since I took his glasses, I became minus ten over time, I guess,' Pagla explained.

'So you never got your eyes tested.'

'No. My dad had got his eyes tested, and he was minus ten in both. I never had a great vision, but when I was hit in the head with a knife, I took my dad's glasses and fit them onto my grandad's frames. It was all blurry initially, but the blurriness has improved over the years.'

This hitting on the head with a knife was always a mystery and kept that way. All that was in public domain was that the knife-head incident happened when he was in Sorbonne.

'So you are carrying the burden of three generations on your nose,' Amal interfered.

'I have no burden at all, and I have no one,' Pagla clarified.

'You have only God to deal with,' Pradipta pointed out. Pagla gazed at the ceiling.

Pradipta first put the recovered glass piece in the earthen tea cup where there was some un-drunk cold tea to cleanse it of mud and dirt. The mud was washed away, but the glass became cloudy and sticky. At this point Chandni assumed charge, taking the glass piece from Pradipta and dipping it in water in an earthen cup brought by the girl. She pressed it back onto the frame, tying the broken stem with a thread and handing it back to Pagla.

With blurry vision restored, Pagla spoke. 'Why couldn't they spare the specs? It beats me!'

ঔ

The beating and the thrashing were quickly forgotten as the night shift focused on the copy at hand. The teleprinter kept up a constant clatter with the tea boy and the copy boy rushing in and out of the dense smoke-filled ten-by-twelve-foot dugout called the newsroom. The copy boy at present was Pradipta who declared he needed some time to clear his head after the clash with the local mafia. Clearing his head meant securing more cigarettes on credit from Banshi and adding to the haze in the room. These days Pradipta had cut down drastically on cigarette intake, especially with Chandni around. But this evening, rules were somehow relaxed. Chandni did not even look once at Pradipta while he was smoking, the way she would usually look prompting Pradipta to stub out his lighted tobacco on the cement floor. The fight outside the office gate had pulled the crowd inside even closer. No one was raising any point, the usual verbal to and fro was missing, and Chandni focused more intently on the Asahi Pentax that Pradipta had given her.

It was the most expensive possession that any of them had. This was widely known as Pradipta's weakness. He had accepted the gadget as a gift years ago from a long-dead relative who had a few of those devices. Over the years he could neither give it away nor accept it as his. The result was it lay mostly inside his bag over the years under a pile of clothes wrapped in a towel. It was a wonder that it was still working when it was given to Chandni.

'Do you know what this is?' Pradipta asked.

Chandni nodded.

After Pradipta explained how the black and silver camera worked, Chandni kept flicking the film advance lever and pressing the shutter for what seemed like hours. The girl took turns in looking through the viewfinder and shooting whatever came in her way.

After about a month of Chandni shooting continuously with a filmless camera with the girl in tow, Amal one day got a Kodak 100 black-and-white roll and loaded it for Chandni. The result was thirty-six frames of mostly frozen newsroom life. A spider behind Pagla's right ear on the wall as he gazed at the ceiling, a whole table of copy and cigarette ash, a hazy Amal with his hands clasped behind his head, and a row of autorickshaws with an old man sleeping in one somewhere in town. The last one was taken on the front page by Amal with the caption 'Sleeping on the job. Picture: Chandni.'

She was quick in turning the distance scale ring, and before anyone could duck out of the frame, she would have taken the shot. Not that too many people refused. Chandni inspired obedience in a rather untamed gathering. Even Dr Avinash gave in to Chandni's demand, posing with an earthen cup of country liquor next to a lilting candle flame.

Majhi walked in, announcing the fire.

'The railway station's burning. Someone has to go,' said Majhi.

Before anyone could react, Chandni had picked up her camera bag and was at the door.

'Pradipta, you better get your head totally cleared and go with Chandni,' said Amal.

'Leave a single column for me and a ten by four for the picture,' said Pradipta, walking out with Chandni.

The fire was enormous and relentless. A lone fire tender threw water in a parabolic curve from outside the station building, which seemed to be encouraging the fire to leap higher into darkness. Two police inspectors leaned against a jeep, watching the orange spectacle along with a crowd of shopkeepers and hangers-on. The unbearable heat kept the crowd at bay, almost five hundred metres from where the tankers were burning.

'Where's Badababu?' Pradipta asked.

The inspector gave an enigmatic smile. 'He's in Dhaniakhali.'

'Where's the stationmaster?' Pradipta pressed on.

'He's also in Dhaniakhali by this time, I guess.'

'Anyone hurt?'

The inspector nodded. Before Pradipta could ask another question, the inspector explained, 'A goods train carrying naptha was waiting at the station, leaking since afternoon. Banwari, who mans the level crossing, went to have a look at it in the evening with a kerosene lamp. He jumped and ran for his life as well.'

Pradipta and Chandni ran up the stairs to the overhead bridge, which was quite a distance from the burning train. But the heat was so intense it was still difficult to stay on the bridge for any length of time. Four coaches burnt fiercely as Chandni lay prostrate on the bridge with Pradipta crouching next to her, vainly trying to shield her from the heat.

They ran quickly down the steps towards the police jeep.

'I thought goods trains carrying petroleum products were not allowed on this section,' Pradipta said.

The inspector turned his head, spat some paan juice on the road, and kept looking.

Pagla had first proposed the leaking train thesis, which no one really understood. 'I couldn't come for the morning shift since the goods train was leaking,' said Pagla.

Amal became curious. 'You mean your train leaked?'

'A tanker, in front of ours. It was leaking diesel or

something. Our train was running at full speed but wouldn't move,' Pagla said, looking up to the ceiling.

Since Pagla's word was usually accepted, there was not much of an argument. Amal was not really convinced that a train would stall on oiled tracks, but he let it pass.

Pagla was tackling the lead on page one. It was better to leave him totally alone at such times. At one thirty in the morning, the anchor and other stories were all in. Except Pagla's. Forty-five minutes later, Pagla passed up the lead on the trade union leader Ram Bhulao's murder and his eventual burial that evening, with a banner heading, 72-point, bold, all caps—RAM BHULAO GOES UNDERGROUND. Even Amal couldn't take it. He screamed, 'Paglaaaaa…'

By the time Pradipta and Chandni reached office, the rest of the stories were in. Amal had kept three columns by fifteen for the fire picture, but when Chandni showed the photographs, Amal wanted to redo the page.

'It's 2.30. Do you really want to do it?' Pradipta hesitated.

'I can't let the pictures go to waste,' said Amal.

In one, the inspector was in silhouette in one corner, spitting paan juice, with grey and white fire and smoke overwhelming the rest of the frame.

'Spitting fire' was the caption subhead given by Pagla.

The other picture was of the dancing figurines of the wrought-iron railings on the overhead bridge embracing the grey-white madness that threatened to devour the station.

'Didn't we have a colour roll?' Amal wanted to know.

Chandni nodded her head.

'Black and white is best. It would have looked filmy in colour,' Pagla thought out aloud.

'You're the finest photojournalist I have seen,' said Amal. 'Can you make me copies of the pictures?'

Chandni nodded again.

ಐಙ

When Pradipta signed off the front page, it was close to four in the morning. The icy wind blew in from the wilderness where Dr Avinash's morgue was. As Pradipta stepped out with Chandni, he felt he was naked underneath the windcheater he had picked up from the border. At 150 rupees, it had looked like a bargain. But Pradipta knew either it was a stolen item or a fake, but it would serve its purpose. He was regretting his decision as Chandni put her light shawl around Pradipta. Pradipta didn't even object since she hardly felt cold.

There was a fire lit with a punctured cycle tyre, dry leaves, and balsa wood outside the tea stall and a small crowd sat around it. Amal was hugging the girl to keep her warm, who was holding on to Amal half asleep. Even Banshi was around, which was not usual, since he opened his shop at seven in the morning.

'Tomorrow I am going to the temple,' said Banshi before Pradipta could ask him. 'Will be here in the evening, babu.'

A fresh saucepan of tea was being made. Water, milk, sugar, and powdered tea were being heated in a bubbly fusion as the crowd around the fire kept a close watch on the process.

The headlight of an approaching scooter made them look the other way.

'Sunil Madhav?' said Pradipta before others could react. It was unusual for the chief reporter to be heading back to office at this hour. He was mostly 'untouchable' after nine in the evening.

'I don't touch liquor in the morning' was his famous comment. 'Liquor touches me at night.'

'Coming from Dr Avinash's,' said Madhav. 'Ram Bhulao's men have hit back. They were just waiting for his funeral. At least a hundred tribals killed in the village near Bada Nullah. The first bodies have come to the morgue.'

There was silence except the crackling of the fire and a jackal calling at a distance.

This time Amal reacted first. 'Bada Nullah could be around sixty kilometres from here.'

'We can't go there now. Better go to the railway hospital where some injured are being sent,' said Madhav. 'And the approach road through the forest is non-existent and deadly at night.'

Chandni had already picked up her camera bag on her shoulders, standing next to Pradipta's scooter.

'How can you come wearing just this shawl?' asked Pradipta, wrapping the shawl around her shoulders. Chandni didn't say a word but just sat on the pillion.

Amal climbed on to Madhav's pillion as the girl stood on the footboard in front of Madhav.

When the group of four plus the girl arrived at the railway hospital, police had cordoned off the emergency gate.

But the inspector had one look at Pradipta's face and let the two scooters in. The deputy commissioner was on the police wireless.

'You can't take pictures here,' he said. Chandni just

walked inside the emergency ward where events unfolded in slow motion. A man was pushing a gurney with a half-naked body on it. He pushed it from one end of the room to the other and then to another corner, looking for a suitable spot to park his trolley. Another man, holding on to a blood-soaked bandage around his half-slit stomach was talking slowly to a medic who was trying to give him an injection. But the man did not seem to be in any kind of obvious pain and even smiled at the camera when Chandni focused on him.

❧

Outside, Pradipta took out his notepad.

'Where was this?' asked Pradipta.

'Jum Jhuma village, next to the Bada Nullah,' said the deputy commissioner, trying to be busy on the wireless.

'How many dead?'

'Possibly hundred, or maybe more.'

'How many injured?'

'Don't know.'

'Who did this? Ram Bhulao's men?' Pradipta pressed on.

'Perhaps. Can't say. Listen, Pradipta-babu, I am very busy. Have to talk to the commissioner. Will talk to you later,' said the deputy commissioner, getting inside the jeep.

A tall young man, with chiselled face and longish hair, in his twenties, was strapped to a cycle rickshaw with ropes. He was talking to himself and sometimes screaming. As Pradipta approached the restrained man, another young man from the small crowd around the rickshaw stepped forward.

'His whole family was slaughtered. A ten-year-old girl, his wife, and parents,' said the man. 'He simply flipped.'

As the tied man let out another roar, piercing the heavens with a scream that seemed from another world, Pradipta asked, 'How did he survive?'

'He hid in the bushes. They killed the men first, raped the women, and then killed them. Most were hacked and then burnt,' said the informer.

'How long did this continue?'

'Several hours. Whole evening. The police came after the village was gutted.'

Chandni was taking a close-up of the tied man. He looked at Chandni and smiled into the camera with the innocence of a ten-year-old who had been let off by his teacher, savouring the first taste of freedom as rain pierced the old banyan tree outside the classroom.

Chandni put her camera in the bag, sitting down on the ground. The girl who was glued to Chandni all this while walked up to the rickshaw and put her hand on the tied forearm. This seemed to calm the man as if he had been given a strong dose of a sleeping medicine. Amal put his arm round the girl and hugged her tightly.

By the time they came back to office, the translucent veil of night was being lifted, with the first rays making a hesitant appearance through a dark-grey overhang. Pradipta pushed the tea man and the tea boy, who were like corpses tightly wrapped in heavy grey blankets to one side and lit the spirit cup in the Primus stove to set it up. Chandni pushed Pradipta aside, pumped vigorously the fuel tank, and placed the saucepan on the stove with the cold tea covered with a fine cloth that had turned chocolate brown. As the tea boiled again, mixed with the first drops of dawn rain seeping in through a hole in the tarpaulin, Pradipta began humming;

A night of known strains mixed with mohua
Drops of a few tears lashed with blood
In the cacophony of unworldly predators
Can you still sleep untouched?
When fire tempers the machetes of death
Dancing untamed with evil clasped
Rivers nameless won't quench dying thirst
Can you still sleep untouched?

A girl played with fatal crimson glow
Arms extended to unmoved gods who watched
Thunder muted, lighting broken in half
Can you still sleep untouched?

ꕥ

Chapter 10

Pagla scratched the walls to get some lime. He mixed the scratched slaked lime from the wall with tobacco leaves and chewed it. Fortunately, no one was around this time of the day. There was an early office meeting from which Pagla was exempted. He always was since he was not considered a management type, which suited him, and left him to his thoughts, scratching and cigarettes. The wall scratching had been discovered a long time ago, and Pagla was warned by Amal that he would be thrown out if it happened again. Pagla took Amal seriously. If it had been Pradipta, Pagla would have thought he could get a second chance. Pradipta issued threats frequently, but he was also flexible. Amal never threatened anyone.

'I didn't expect this. If this happens again, you will not be here,' said Amal.

This was at least ten months ago, and Pagla had kept his promise so far. But today was different. The beating, which he received the previous week, had left him with a recurrent pain in his left shoulder. He hadn't told anyone about that. And in any case, he knew no one had the money to get him treated in a private clinic. He could go to the hospital some twenty miles away, stand in a queue the whole day, and be seen by a doctor or an intern who might have given him the wrong drugs to make matters worse. He never believed anyone was ever treated in the Murigram hospital, known as the halfway house to the crematorium.

It was not that Pagla was in any way averse to the crematorium. He just believed it was the wrong way to go. The road to the burning ghat should be straight and narrow and at least not through the hospital. On some days, in the afternoon when he was not being hounded by piles of teleprinter copy, he would walk to the riverbank where the last embers of a dying pyre would give him solace. A stray dog would slowly crawl up, sitting next to him. Some days, if he was lucky, Chuni Lal would appear from the forest, enticing him with a half bottle of chullu. As the heat rose to forty degrees plus, the wind singed the skin on his back, he would take off the woollen jumper he wore on such occasions and feel free. He liked the heat, dust and ash, which filled him with a sense of purity—he didn't know why. The rain pushed him more indoors and deep inside his own being, making him more reluctant to talk, let alone do anything else. That was one reason Pagla hardly ever had a bath.

As Chuni Lal dangled the chullu in front of him, as if it were a red cloth luring a raging bull, Pagla said, 'Wait.'

He got up slowly and fished out a crumpled cigarette from his shirt pocket, walking to the heap of black ashes and darkened pieces of bones. He lay prostrate on the ground, the cigarette on his lips, inching closer to the last red twig lying in the ashes. As the cigarette touched the burning twig, Pagla inhaled deeply and stood up.

Taking a small sip of chullu, he returned the bottle. 'Amal will kill you, not me.'

'Won't tell him. Just one more sip,' Chuni Lal said.

'You keep that for the night. I have page one to worry about,' Pagla said, putting his hand around Chuni Lal's shoulders as the two made their way back from their afternoon sojourn at the burning ghat.

Amal saw the new scratchings. 'Again?'

'You were not supposed to be back,' said Pagla. 'I can promise . . .'

Pradipta walked in, taking a while to comprehend the scene in front of him. Pagla and Amal were standing next to a wall, saying nothing.

'Pagla has to do the water board story,' said Pradipta, breaking the silence. 'Sunil Madhav said no one would open up to him. With Pagla, they might feel freer.'

'What about the night shift?' asked Amal.

'I will manage,' said Pradipta. 'Pagla, talk to Sunil Madhav now. I want the story by ten. It might be a lead.' As the trio headed back to office, Pagla gave Amal his half-smoked cigarette, which he accepted quietly.

❧

Sunil Madhav was on the phone, feet up on a chair. Chandni scrutinized the black-and-white prints that she had developed the day before.

Pradipta hugged Chandni from behind. 'If we have such pictures, we don't need Pagla's rubbish copy.' Chandni looked up at Pradipta and smiled.

'Rubbish sells. And the paper is used to cover up rubbish in any case,' Pagla pointed out softly.

'The paper is used to wrap up shoes, especially muddy ones,' clarified Pradipta.

'After ten minutes, thirty seconds, that is the lifespan of a newspaper,' said Amal.

No one knew how Amal could predict the life and death of a newspaper with such precision, but it was generally agreed that the lifespan of a newspaper was very short, counted in minutes, even that of *The Murigram Post* for which they were ready to die.

Sunil Madhav explained the shots to Chandni.

'The two guys shouldn't be recognizable. Take the shots from behind. Their heads must be covered in a shawl. And take your tripod along. You can't use flash,' said Sunil Madhav.

'Can we take them in candlelight?' asked Pagla.

'Yes, if she has any 400 film left. Maybe,' said Sunil Madhav.

Chandni nodded, indicating she had one roll of Kodak 400.

ઊ

The wind began to pick up speed, along with a few drops of rain, when the reporting team set out in the evening. Chandni and Pagla rode pillion with Sunil Madhav and Pradipta. Words were hardly exchanged as the four wound their way through the chaotic town traffic and reached the water board office, which was situated next to a cone-shaped concrete water tank placed atop tall concrete columns.

The office was a single-storey block made up of a cluster of rooms, which were linked to each other with no apparent thought or design. Large green painted wooden doors separated the rooms. The room of the chairman of the board was on the right, next to a flight of stairs that led to a small cemented porch. A thick green cotton curtain, which had turned greenish brown from heat and dust, hung from a coiled metal spring at the chairman's door. A brass name plaque was loosely hanging from a screw at one end on the door. It was Saturday evening; the rooms were padlocked, with only a hundred-watt naked bulb hanging from a green wire keeping watch over a forlorn porch that was completely bare and clean.

As the two scooters were parked outside the porch and the four climbed the few steps, the swinging light from the ceiling started a cinema of gigantic shadows on the chairman's office wall. Chandni sat on the porch floor, loading her Pentax with the last roll of high-speed Kodak she had preserved for a long time. Pradipta sat at one end on the stairs, Pagla lay on his back, and Sunil Madhav leant against the wall. A dark young man in his twenties approached the reporting team from the shadows. He was the water pump operator—tall and well-built in greyish trousers and a white vest, wearing rubber slippers and *rudraksha* beads around his neck. As he came near, Sunil Madhav walked up to him, and without exchanging a word, the duo set off towards the one-room, one-window tenement where the pump operator lived with his wife and two young children. Chandni and Pagla caught up with Sunil Madhav as two other figures soon became visible in the shadows behind the tenement.

'You will never be identified,' assured Pagla.

'What if you are told to reveal sources?' one of them asked.

'I will go to jail instead,' Pagla promised. 'We will take your pictures just from the back.'

Chandni placed the camera on a broken ledge as Pagla took notes. Pradipta and Sunil Madhav and the pump operator stood about ten feet from Pagla and the water board sources.

Chandni lit two candles and asked Pagla to hold them. It took much effort by all present to keep the candles burning in the wind.

'How much has been changing hand?' asked Pagla.

'Lakhs,' said one of the sources, handing over a sheaf of papers to Pagla.

'For how long?'

'For more than five years, since this chairman took over.'

ଔଓ

Water was a precious commodity in Murigram. How water was supplied to many small and big industrial units dotting the landscape went a long way towards the survival of businesses. Not surprisingly, the chairman and some water board officials led a very comfortable life. Pagla's front-page lead story ran with the headline given by Pradipta, 'Water Stains Mar Board Officials' with a subhead asking 'Why are some units flooded and others going dry?' Chandni provided a six-column picture anchoring the story, framed by the silhouettes of two men in candlelight with the dark outlines of a looming water tank etched against the sky.

The newsroom assumed a lighter mood in the forenoon, with calls coming in praise of the exposé with Pagla staring at the ceiling with his knees pressing against the desk.

'The impact would be short-term,' said Sunil Madhav.

'Will they launch a probe?' asked Amal, offering Pagla a cigarette.

'I doubt it,' said Sunil Madhav, 'Chandni's imagery is having more impact than the story, I guess. All copies sold out at the market.'

The phone rang again.

'Mr Amal?'

'Yes.'

'Tears will flow.' The caller hung up before Amal could respond.

'Sunil, can you ask Anil Singh to take note of a threat against the paper,' said Amal.

'What kind of threat?' asked Pradipta.

'Tears will flow,' said Amal.

Pagla sent three smoke rings aimed at the ceiling before joining the discussion. 'If water flows, can tears be far behind?' The laughter submerged the animated exchange Sunil Madhav had with the police chief.

ઉ෴ഩ

It was an unusually clear evening with the first hint of an incoming winter. The perfectly rounded moon stood on top of the *shimul* tree that guarded Banshi's shop. Pagla breathed in the cool air, which always lifted his spirits since he had even less reason to go near water. Every year when the severe winter set in, Pagla became more productive, subbing two copies instead of one every evening, and his usual brief sentences became a little elongated. Amal even had a theory that the fall in temperature was directly proportional to the length of Pagla's speech.

'Moon, not money, grows on trees,' said Pagla, noticing Chandni following closely behind.

As Pagla reached Banshi's shop, the motorbike pulled up next to him.

'Pagla?' asked the man riding on the pillion. Before he could reply, the first bullet went through his head above the temple. As he slumped to the ground, a second bullet went through his chest, lodging at the foot of the tree.

'Swines. They have killed Pagla,' screamed Chandni, running towards the man sprawled in the dirt. Banshi jumped down from his shop with Chandni cradling Pagla's head, her tears merging with the red fluid flowing from the fresh wound. Pagla's thick lenses, bloodied and dirty, remained intact, safely lodged at the foot of the tree.

The procession was long and unusually quiet. Even the dog ran ahead of the crowd without making a noise. Dr Avinash was in front, carrying the wooden cot on his right shoulder. Amal was on his right. Pradipta and Chandni supported the rear of the cot. In between there was Banshi on one side and Sunil Madhav and Ranen on the other. Chuni Lal and Parasin were five steps ahead of the cot bearers. Pagla was in deep slumber, with his glasses on, gazing at the limitless sky. The rounded silvery moon, a day older, had turned into a fiery orange, way above the shimul. As the marchers entered Parasin's colony, hundreds joined the procession.

No one smoked. There was no hint of the usual chullu. Only Dr Avinash's deep baritone rose.

The shop's shut long ago amid sleepless night
Naked light dwindled in corrugated sheet
The new breeze rising from darkened east
Distant madol faltered with river's beat
Wares spread on dishevelled porch
Clay cups clustered with burnt pot
Untouched leaves
There's no need to wait for me
Beside the old shimul
Amid the dishevelled porch

Chandni's deep, melodious voice also rose for the first time.

I'm with you,
Maybe not now.
I'm sunk in your ocean eyes,
Maybe not now.
I'm wrapped in your serenity,
Maybe not now.
How could you turn away,
Believing in now!
Long before the sun rose, we met.
Long after we forget, we'll float together.
There's no change in million specks above,
Nor in your falling hair,
Nor in your arching grasp,
Like the immutable bent space.
We exist before and after.
How could you turn away,
Believing in now!

ꕥ

www.ingramcontent.com/pod-product-compliance
Lightning Source LLC
LaVergne TN
LVHW011047110826
845149LV00015B/3396

* 9 7 8 8 1 9 3 9 5 0 4 7 0 *